Skeletals Rituals:
Adventures to
the
Heart of the Underworld

Author/Publisher: B. A. Harris Publishing's

To my Amazing Family Friends and Medical Team

Thank you for being there for me in my darkest hour. If not for you all,
I would not be here

Disclaimer

The views and opinions expressed in this book are those of the author and do not necessarily reflect the official policy or position of any distributor, manufacturer, or affiliated organization. The content is intended for informational and entertainment purposes only. The publisher, B. A. Harris Publishing's , and the author accept no responsibility for any errors or omissions, or for any consequences resulting from the use of the information contained in this book.

The views and opinions expressed in the content published by B. A. Harris Publishing's , including books, cartoons, comic books, video games, mobile games, music beats and lyrics, art, and poetry, are those of the individual creators and do not necessarily reflect the official policy or position of B. A. Harris Publishing's or any of its affiliates. All content is provided "as is" without warranty of any kind, either express or implied, including but not limited to the implied warranties of merchantability, fitness for a particular purpose, or non-infringement.

B. A. Harris Publishing's is not responsible for any errors or omissions, or for the results obtained from the use of this information. Any action you take upon the information found in the content published by B. A. Harris Publishing's is strictly at your own risk, and B. A. Harris Publishing's will not be liable for any losses or damages in connection with the use of our content.

Distributors

The opinions expressed in this book are solely those of the author and are not endorsed or affiliated with any distributors or manufacturers.

Table of Contents

Prologue: Land of the Living Dead

In the shadowy depths of the Underworld, where the light of the sun was but a distant memory, a realm thrived in endless revelry. The Land of the Living Dead was a place where every day was a festival and every night a masquerade. Skeletons, phantoms, and spirits danced in harmony, their ceaseless celebration echoing through the twilight air. In this eerie yet jubilant world, existence was a carnival of eternal joy.

Among the revelers was the Skeleton Man, a figure whose bones, though worn, clattered rhythmically with the beat of the endless festivities. He moved gracefully among the throng, his hollow eye sockets shimmering with the faint glow of otherworldly light. His existence had always been a blend of mirth and monotony, a cycle of amusement without end. The Land of the Living Dead was a realm of perpetual celebration, but for the Skeleton Man, the revelry had become a dull routine.

One day, while meandering through the bustling heart of the Underworld's grand festival, he stumbled upon an unusual sight. Tucked away in a dusty corner of an old, forgotten bookstore was a comic book, its cover vibrant and striking amidst the drab surroundings. The title, "The Mighty Guardian," gleamed with a promise of heroism and adventure. Intrigued, Skeleton Man picked up the comic, his skeletal fingers tracing the cover's intricate design.

As he delved into the pages, the world around him seemed to fade. The comic's hero, a bold figure clad in bright, flowing attire, was celebrated as a savior of the world. He fought evil, overcame great challenges, and was adored by millions. Each page brimmed with thrilling exploits and triumphant victories. The Skeleton Man's hollow eyes widened with each turn, captivated by the notion of a life beyond endless parties and festivities.

The more he read, the more a longing stirred within him. He dreamed of heroism, of making a difference in a world where his actions could mean something profound. The thought of adventure, of saving lives and experiencing new things, filled him with a restless energy he hadn't felt in centuries. The idea that someone like him—though skeletal and from the Land of the Living Dead—could become a hero in the Land of the Living ignited a spark within him.

Determined, the Skeleton Man set down the comic book with newfound resolve. "I will return to the world," he vowed quietly to himself. "I will become a superhero who marries the beautiful woman and finally have something new to do for an eternity." The promise of a new purpose beckoned, and the allure of a life beyond the ceaseless revelry was irresistible.

As the last echoes of the Underworld's celebration faded into the distance, Skeleton Man began to prepare for his journey. Little did he know, the Land of the Living was a world very different from the one he had left behind, and his path to becoming a hero would be fraught with challenges he could not yet imagine. But with determination and hope, he set forth from the Land of the Living Dead, ready to embrace his destiny in the world of the living.

Skeleton Man's departure from the Land of the Living Dead was met with a mix of curiosity and amusement from the other denizens. Some chuckled at the idea of one of their own seeking fame and glory in the Land of the Living, while others wished him well, intrigued by his audacious plan.

As he crossed the boundary between the Underworld and the world above, a strange sensation enveloped him—both exhilarating and disorienting. The vibrant, ever-changing landscape of the Land of the Living was a stark contrast to the perpetual twilight of his former home. He marveled at the colors, the sounds, and the bustling energy of the city that lay before him.

Skeleton Man spent weeks preparing for his new role. He practiced flying, mastering his agility, and fine-tuned his combat skills with the fervor of someone eager to prove themselves. His days were filled with rigorous training, while his nights were spent designing a superhero costume that would be both functional and emblematic of his undead heritage. The result was a striking ensemble: a sleek, dark suit adorned with bone-like accents, a flowing cape that fluttered with an ethereal glow, and a mask that concealed his skeletal visage while adding an air of mystery.

With his costume complete and his training nearly at an end, Skeleton Man felt a surge of excitement and trepidation. He stood atop a high building, gazing at the sprawling city below, his skeletal heart pounding with anticipation. The time had come to make his debut and put his newfound purpose into action.

However, as he descended into the streets, the reception he received was far from what he had imagined. His eerie appearance, while majestic in the Underworld, was met with screams, panic, and a hasty retreat from the citizens of the Land of the Living. His attempts to help were met with fear rather than gratitude, and his heroic gestures were misinterpreted as threats.

News of the "Skeleton Superhero" spread quickly, but not in the way he had hoped. Instead of being celebrated, he became a source of anxiety and ridicule. The city buzzed with gossip and speculation about this unsettling new figure. Some saw him as a ghastly menace, while others were simply bewildered by his strange presence.

The Skeleton Man's initial attempts at heroism were met with confusion and hostility. His efforts to thwart petty crimes and assist those in need were overshadowed by his terrifying appearance. Each encounter seemed to reinforce his status as an outsider, a figure of fear rather than a beacon of hope.

Despite the setbacks, Skeleton Man remained resolute. The dream of becoming a celebrated hero, of experiencing love and purpose beyond the confines of his former life, kept him moving forward. He knew the path to acceptance would be arduous, fraught with misunderstandings and challenges, but his determination was unwavering.

As he wandered through the city, grappling with the cold reception and the growing distance between his dreams and reality, Skeleton Man clung to the hope that one day, he would bridge the gap between the Land of the Living and the Land of the Living Dead. He was ready to face whatever trials awaited him, driven by the belief that true heroism meant enduring hardship and proving oneself worthy of a place in the world he had chosen to join.

In this new world, where every step was a challenge and every action was scrutinized, Skeleton Man set forth with a resolve as strong as the bones that comprised his form. His journey had only just begun, and the path to becoming a true superhero in the Land of the Living was filled with uncertainty and trials. But with courage and perseverance, he was determined to transform his dream into reality and find his place among the living.

The first few weeks in the Land of the Living were a whirlwind of confusion and frustration for Skeleton Man. He had envisioned a grand entrance, a triumphant debut where people would cheer and celebrate his arrival as a new hero. Instead, he found himself dodging frightened bystanders and evading the police who mistook him for a threat.

Every night, as he retreated to a hidden rooftop or a darkened alley, the weight of his disillusionment pressed heavily upon him. The city's vibrant lights and bustling energy seemed distant and unwelcoming, a stark contrast to the ceaseless celebration of his former home. His attempts to help, whether rescuing a cat from a tree or stopping a mugging, were met with terror rather than gratitude.

In the midst of this turmoil, Skeleton Man found solace in his nightly routine of studying the comic book that had inspired him. He poured over its pages, drawing strength from the superhero's unwavering resolve and heroic deeds. The superhero's charisma and success served as a beacon of hope, reminding Skeleton Man of the dreams he had left behind in the Underworld.

One fateful evening, as Skeleton Man grappled with his growing sense of isolation, he encountered an unexpected ally. Amidst a chaotic scene where he tried to prevent a carjacking, a young woman—brave and compassionate—stepped in to assist him. Unlike others, she did not flee in fear but instead faced the situation with a calm demeanor and a hopeful gaze.

Her name was Eliza, and she had always been an advocate for those who were misunderstood. She saw something in Skeleton Man that others did not—a genuine desire to help and an earnest heart. She approached him cautiously but without fear, extending a hand of friendship and understanding.

"Eliza, I'm... I'm trying to be a hero," Skeleton Man confessed, his voice tinged with both pride and desperation. "But everything is so different here. No one seems to want my help."

Eliza listened intently, her eyes reflecting both empathy and curiosity. "I believe you have the potential to be a hero, but the world needs to see past your appearance. They need to understand that your intentions are pure."

With Eliza's encouragement, Skeleton Man began to find a glimmer of hope. She introduced him to small community groups and local organizations, helping him to connect with those who might be more open to his unconventional form of heroism. Through these interactions, he slowly started to gain a measure of acceptance.

Eliza's support did more than just offer practical advice; it provided Skeleton Man with the emotional strength he needed to persevere. As they spent more time together, their bond deepened. Skeleton Man found himself drawn to Eliza's kindness and resilience, and for the first time since his arrival, he began to believe that his dreams might be achievable.

The city's response began to shift gradually. While there were still skeptics and those who remained wary of the Skeleton Superhero, more people started to see him not as a grotesque oddity but as a symbol of hope and determination. He began to make a real impact, helping in ways that went beyond mere physical heroics—offering support to those in need, providing a sense of security, and becoming a fixture in the community.

As the weeks turned into months, Skeleton Man's journey transformed from one of rejection to one of cautious acceptance. His dream of becoming a celebrated hero was still a work in progress, but with Eliza by his side and a growing number of allies, he was making strides toward achieving it. The Land of the Living, though still challenging and complex, was beginning to open up to him in ways he had never anticipated.

The prologue of Skeleton Man's story thus set the stage for a tale of perseverance, transformation, and the search for acceptance in a world that was initially hostile but gradually becoming more inclusive. With each passing day, he inched closer to realizing his dreams, driven by the hope that, despite his origins, he could find a place where he truly belonged.

Chapter 1: A Hero's Welcome

The city of Crestwood bustled with its usual frenetic energy. Tall skyscrapers stretched toward the sky, their glass facades reflecting the neon glow of countless advertisements and streetlights. The hum of traffic and the chatter of pedestrians created a cacophony that filled the urban landscape. Amidst this vibrant cityscape, a lone figure stood out—Skeleton Man, now a visible presence in the Land of the Living.

His first weeks had been marked by a series of trials. His appearance, both unique and unsettling, continued to evoke fear and skepticism. The public's reaction ranged from screams of terror to hurried phone calls to the authorities. He had tried to make a positive impact, rescuing a lost dog, helping an elderly woman with her groceries, and intervening in minor crimes. Yet, every attempt seemed to only reinforce his status as an outsider.

On this particular day, Skeleton Man was determined to prove himself. He had received word of a criminal gang operating in Crestwood, involved in a series of high-profile heists. The local news had reported their latest crime—a daring theft of valuable artifacts from the Crestwood Museum. Skeleton Man saw this as an opportunity to demonstrate his heroism and make a meaningful contribution to the city.

He carefully scouted the museum, observing the security measures and the patterns of the guards. From the shadows of an alley, he watched as the museum's staff and police discussed their next steps. His bone-white figure, partially concealed by his flowing cape, remained hidden from view. The plan was straightforward: he would thwart the criminals' escape and recover the stolen artifacts.

As night fell, Skeleton Man took his position near the museum's main entrance. The streets were quieter now, the crowds having dissipated into the evening. He knew that timing was crucial. As the clock struck midnight, he saw the gang's van approach, its headlights cutting through the darkness.

With swift, calculated movements, Skeleton Man launched into action. He dashed toward the van, his movements a blend of eerie elegance and deadly precision. The gang members, caught off guard, scrambled in panic as he appeared from the shadows. A brief struggle ensued, with Skeleton Man using his agility and strength to disarm and incapacitate the robbers.

Despite his efforts, the confrontation quickly turned chaotic. The gang members, bewildered and frightened by his skeletal form, reacted with unpredictable aggression. Their screams and desperate pleas only added to the pandemonium. The sound of approaching sirens grew louder, and the fear in the criminals' eyes mirrored that of the onlookers who had gathered nearby.

In the midst of the commotion, a familiar face emerged from the crowd—Eliza. Her expression was one of both concern and resolve. She approached Skeleton Man, her presence a beacon of support in the chaotic scene. She shouted over the noise, "You're doing great! Just hold them until the police arrive!"

With Eliza's encouragement, Skeleton Man renewed his efforts. He worked to subdue the remaining gang members, his actions driven by a fierce determination to protect the city. As the police arrived and began to take control of the situation, they were met with a mix of astonished and skeptical looks from the crowd.

The police officers, having seen the chaos and the strange figure responsible for it, were cautious but professional. They secured the scene and began to question the witnesses. Skeleton Man, standing at the periphery, was aware of their wary glances. The mixed reception from the public and the authorities left him feeling both triumphant and uncertain.

Eliza approached him as the police worked to clean up the scene. "You did well tonight," she said with a reassuring smile. "The museum will recover the artifacts, and the criminals are off the streets. You're making a difference."

Skeleton Man nodded, his hollow eye sockets reflecting a glimmer of hope. "Thank you, Eliza. I just hope the city can see past my appearance and recognize my intentions."

As the crowd dispersed and the city returned to its normal rhythm, Skeleton Man and Eliza walked away from the museum. The night had been a challenging one, but it marked a significant step in his journey. For the first time, he felt a sense of accomplishment and acceptance, however small it might be.

Eliza glanced at him with a mixture of admiration and empathy. "It's going to take time, but you're on the right path. Keep doing what you're doing, and eventually, people will see you for who you truly are—a hero."

As Skeleton Man looked up at the city skyline, he felt a renewed sense of purpose. The road to acceptance would be long and fraught with obstacles, but with Eliza's support and his own unwavering resolve, he was ready to continue his quest. The journey had only just begun, and the Land of the Living awaited his next move.

As the night wore on and the city slowly settled back into its familiar rhythm, Eliza and Skeleton Man found a quiet corner in a nearby park. The adrenaline of the earlier confrontation had subsided, and the two stood in a momentary respite, the cool night air filling the space between them.

Eliza looked at Skeleton Man with curiosity and concern. "You know," she began tentatively, "I've been wondering about you. You've done a lot to help tonight, and I think you're really making a difference. But I don't know much about you. What's your real name?"

Skeleton Man's skeletal visage turned toward her, the hollow eye sockets reflecting the soft light of the park's lampposts. For a moment, he was silent, lost in thought. The question seemed to stir something deep within him—a memory, a fragment of a past long forgotten.

"I... don't remember," he admitted quietly, his voice tinged with melancholy. "I'm hundreds of years old. I've lost track of time. My real name, my past life—it's all a blur. My headstone has crumbled to dust long ago. The only thing I know is that I was once someone, but that person is now a distant shadow."

Eliza's eyes softened with understanding. She reached out and placed a comforting hand on his skeletal shoulder. "That sounds incredibly difficult. To have such a rich history and yet not be able to recall it... It must be frustrating."

Skeleton Man nodded slowly. "It is. When I was in the Land of the Living Dead, time was... different. We celebrated and lived in an eternal moment. But now, in the Land of the Living, time is linear, and it feels like I've lost a part of myself."

Eliza pondered this revelation. "If you don't remember your past, then perhaps you can create a new identity for yourself here. You're not defined by what you've forgotten. You have the chance to be someone new, someone who makes a positive impact on the world."

He looked at her, a glimmer of hope flickering in his hollow eyes. "That's a comforting thought. I suppose I can't change what's been lost, but I can shape what's ahead of me."

Eliza smiled warmly. "Exactly. And who knows? Maybe in this new life, you'll find new things to remember—new experiences, new connections, and maybe even a new name that suits the hero you're becoming."

Skeleton Man considered her words, finding solace in the idea of starting anew. The weight of his forgotten past seemed a little lighter in the company of someone who genuinely cared. He realized that while his origins might remain shrouded in mystery, his actions moving forward could define who he was becoming.

As the night deepened, Eliza and Skeleton Man continued their conversation, sharing stories and aspirations. For the first time since arriving in the Land of the Living, Skeleton Man felt a sense of belonging, however tentative it might be. Eliza's presence and support offered a glimmer of hope in his quest for acceptance and purpose.

When the conversation finally came to a natural end, Eliza stood up, brushing off her coat. "I need to head back, but I'm glad we had this talk. Remember, you're making a difference, even if it doesn't always feel that way."

Skeleton Man nodded, feeling a renewed sense of determination. "Thank you, Eliza. I won't forget your kindness."

As Eliza walked away into the night, Skeleton Man remained in the park, looking up at the star-filled sky. The city below continued its restless dance, but for the first time, Skeleton Man felt a deeper connection to it. His journey was far from over, and the path ahead remained uncertain, but he was no longer alone.

With a newfound resolve, Skeleton Man set his sights on the future, ready to continue his quest for heroism and acceptance. His past might have been lost to time, but his present and future were filled with possibilities, and he was determined to make the most of them.

As days turned into weeks, Skeleton Man and Eliza's bond grew stronger. The park, where they had shared their first deep conversation, became their regular meeting spot. Their interactions evolved from brief exchanges of gratitude to heartfelt discussions about their dreams, fears, and aspirations. The quiet moments they shared became a sanctuary for both of them—a place where Skeleton Man could be more than just a figure of fear and Eliza could be herself without pretense.

One crisp autumn evening, as the leaves crunched underfoot and the city lights flickered in the distance, Eliza and Skeleton Man sat together on a park bench. The cool breeze rustled the branches overhead, and the atmosphere was filled with a serene calm. Skeleton Man had just returned from another round of attempts to help the citizens of Crestwood, and Eliza had come to hear about his experiences.

"I had another encounter today," Skeleton Man said, his voice carrying a mix of frustration and determination. "I tried to help a group of kids who were being harassed by some bullies. They were so scared they ran away, and the bullies ended up laughing at me."

Eliza listened attentively, her expression one of sympathy and encouragement. "I'm sorry to hear that. It's tough when people react with fear rather than gratitude. But you're making progress. I can see it. People are starting to notice you, even if they're still unsure."

Skeleton Man sighed, looking out at the park's peaceful scenery. "I just wish there was something more I could do to bridge the gap. I want to be seen as a hero, not just a frightening figure."

Eliza's gaze softened as she turned to him. "You know, there's one thing you haven't done yet that might help. Have you thought about giving yourself a new name? Something that reflects who you are and what you're trying to be?"

The suggestion struck Skeleton Man with both surprise and hope. "A new name? I haven't considered that. My past is so far behind me that I never thought about creating a new identity."

Eliza smiled warmly. "It could be a fresh start. A name that captures your heroism and the positive impact you want to make. Something that people can associate with bravery and compassion rather than fear."

Skeleton Man mulled over the idea, his bony fingers drumming thoughtfully on the park bench. "I suppose a new name could help. But what should it be? I'm not exactly sure what would suit me."

Eliza's eyes sparkled with enthusiasm as she leaned closer. "Let's brainstorm together. What about something that symbolizes strength, hope, or renewal? Maybe something that hints at your unique nature but also highlights your heroic qualities?"

They spent the next hour discussing potential names, each suggestion carefully considered and weighed. Eliza's creativity flowed as she came up with ideas like "Bone Guardian," "Eternal Sentinel," and "Spectral Savior." Skeleton Man listened, intrigued by each possibility but still feeling a sense of uncertainty.

As they talked, Eliza's laughter and warmth began to dissolve some of Skeleton Man's insecurities. He found himself increasingly drawn to her kindness and the way she genuinely cared about his quest. Her presence had become a source of comfort and inspiration, and he realized how much he valued their growing friendship.

After much deliberation, Eliza's face lit up with an idea. "How about 'Graveyard Phantom'? It combines the essence of your mysterious, ethereal presence with the courage and strength you show in your actions."

Skeleton Man's hollow eyes brightened as he considered the name. "Graveyard Phantom. I like it. It feels like a name that reflects both my past and my new purpose. Thank you, Eliza."

Eliza smiled, feeling a sense of accomplishment in helping Skeleton Man find a new identity. "You're welcome, Graveyard Phantom. I think it's a name that will resonate with people. It captures both the essence of who you are and the hero you're striving to become."

As the evening wore on and the park's tranquility enveloped them, Skeleton Man felt a renewed sense of hope. With his new name, Graveyard Phantom, he felt as though he had taken a significant step toward integrating himself into the world he now inhabited.

Eliza and Graveyard Phantom walked together through the park, their conversation flowing easily as the night grew darker. The bond between them deepened, their mutual respect and admiration blossoming into something more profound. As they said their goodbyes, Graveyard Phantom felt a sense of contentment and anticipation for the future.

Eliza's influence had given him a new perspective, and with his new name, he was ready to face the challenges ahead. As he watched her walk away into the night, Graveyard Phantom knew that his journey was far from over, but he now had a clearer sense of purpose and a friend who believed in him. The road to becoming a true hero was still long, but he was no longer walking it alone.

Chapter 2: Graveyard Phantom

The first rays of dawn filtered through the tall buildings of Crestwood, casting long shadows over the city. The hustle and bustle of the morning routine began as people stirred awake, unaware of the unusual hero who was about to make his first real attempt at changing their perception. Graveyard Phantom —formerly known only as Skeleton Man—was ready to embrace his new identity.

The park, once a sanctuary for quiet conversations, now served as the training ground for Graveyard Phantom . He had spent countless hours perfecting his superhero costume, which combined elements of his skeletal form with modern superhero aesthetics. The result was an imposing yet sleek suit, adorned with glowing accents that gave him a spectral aura. He had hoped that the new look would help alleviate some of the fear he had encountered.

Eliza arrived at the park, her eyes widening with admiration as she took in the sight of Graveyard Phantom in his full attire. "Wow, you look incredible," she said, her voice filled with genuine enthusiasm. "This is definitely going to make a statement."

Graveyard Phantom adjusted the cape, which flowed gracefully behind him. "Thank you, Eliza. I've been working hard on this. I hope it helps me to connect with people more effectively."

Eliza walked alongside him as he prepared to leave for his first official patrol. "I'm sure it will. You've put so much effort into this, and it shows. Just remember, even if people react with fear initially, your actions will speak louder than your appearance."

With a determined nod, Graveyard Phantom set off into the city. His first destination was a local community center known for its after-school programs and neighborhood outreach. He hoped to make a positive impression by offering assistance and protection to the community.

As Graveyard Phantom approached the community center, he saw a group of children playing in the park nearby. He decided to start small and approached them with a friendly wave. "Hello, kids! I'm Graveyard Phantom . I'm here to help and keep you safe."

The children, initially curious, quickly recoiled in fear as they saw his skeletal visage and eerie glow. They screamed and ran, seeking refuge behind their parents, who stared at Graveyard Phantom with a mixture of apprehension and confusion.

Graveyard Phantom's heart sank. He had hoped for a warmer reception, but the fear in their eyes was unmistakable. He sighed and continued to the community center, where he hoped his presence might be more appreciated.

Inside the center, he met with the director, a middle-aged woman named Mrs. Harrison. She looked at him with a mix of skepticism and curiosity. "I appreciate your offer to help, but we've had some issues with security lately. If you're here to assist, then please, feel free to start by patrolling the perimeter."

Graveyard Phantom nodded, grateful for the opportunity to contribute. He patrolled the area diligently, his senses attuned to any signs of trouble. As he moved through the streets, he noticed a few small incidents: a street performer being hassled by rowdy teens, a car with a flat tire, and a stray dog searching for food. Despite his best efforts, his attempts to assist were met with fear or indifference.

The day wore on, and Graveyard Phantom found himself in a state of frustration. His desire to help was strong, but the fear he evoked in people seemed to overshadow his intentions. As evening approached, he returned to the park, feeling disheartened.

Eliza arrived as the sun began to set, noticing the troubled expression on Graveyard Phantom's face. "How did it go?" she asked, her voice gentle.

Graveyard Phantom shrugged, his skeletal shoulders slumping. "Not as well as I hoped. Everywhere I went, people were afraid. I tried to help, but it seems that no matter how much I want to make a difference, my appearance is a constant barrier."

Eliza sat down next to him on the park bench, her expression thoughtful. "You know, making a difference takes time. It's not just about what you look like; it's about what you do. People will come to see past your exterior when they see your heart and your dedication."

Graveyard Phantom looked at her, feeling a renewed sense of determination. "You're right. I can't give up. I have to keep trying, even if it's hard. I have to prove that I'm more than just my appearance."

Eliza smiled encouragingly. "Exactly. And you don't have to do it alone. You've got me to support you. Maybe we can come up with a plan to gradually show people who you really are and what you stand for."

Graveyard Phantom's eyes brightened at the thought. "That sounds like a good idea. I'd appreciate any help you can offer."

Over the next few weeks, Eliza and Graveyard Phantom worked together to devise a strategy for better integrating him into the community. They organized small events, such as neighborhood cleanups and safety workshops, where Graveyard Phantom could participate without overwhelming people. Eliza used her connections to spread the word about Graveyard Phantom's positive intentions, emphasizing his dedication to helping others.

Slowly but surely, the community began to warm to Graveyard Phantom. Children no longer fled in terror at his approach; instead, they were curious and even began to ask him questions about his powers and his mission. The local residents started to see him not just as a strange figure but as someone who genuinely cared about their well-being.

One day, while walking through the park, Eliza and Graveyard Phantom encountered a young woman named Lily, who had been a victim of a recent mugging. Lily had been reluctant to accept help from anyone, but seeing Graveyard Phantom's efforts in the community, she was willing to give him a chance.

"Thank you for being here," Lily said, her voice shaky but appreciative. "I've seen you around, and while I was scared at first, I see now that you're trying to make a difference. I could use some help."

Graveyard Phantom smiled, his skeletal face softening. "I'm here to help. Let's make sure you're safe and find a way to address what happened."

As Graveyard Phantom continued to support Lily and others like her, his presence became a beacon of hope rather than fear. His dedication and persistence began to pay off, and the city started to embrace him as a genuine hero.

By the end of the month, Graveyard Phantom had made significant strides in his quest to be accepted. His efforts had begun to earn him respect, and his new name had started to resonate with those he helped. The city was slowly learning to see past his exterior and recognize the heart of a true hero.

Eliza watched with pride as Graveyard Phantom's journey unfolded. Their friendship had deepened, and she had come to admire his resilience and determination. As they sat together in the park, enjoying a rare moment of tranquility, Eliza spoke up.

"You're doing great, Graveyard Phantom . I'm really proud of how far you've come."

Graveyard Phantom looked at her with gratitude. "Thank you, Eliza. Your support has meant more to me than I can express. I couldn't have done it without you."

As they watched the sun set over Crestwood, both Eliza and Graveyard Phantom felt a sense of hope and accomplishment. The journey ahead was still uncertain, but they were facing it together, ready to tackle the challenges and embrace the victories that awaited them.

The days continued to pass, and Graveyard Phantom's efforts to integrate himself into the community began to show tangible results. The initial fear that had once greeted him was gradually being replaced by curiosity and, in some cases, appreciation. However, his persistent presence in the park during his off-hours had not gone unnoticed by Eliza, who was increasingly concerned for his well-being.

One evening, as they sat together on the park bench, Eliza looked at Graveyard Phantom with a mix of sympathy and resolve. "You know, Graveyard Phantom , I've been thinking. You've been living out here in the park for quite some time, and while it's great that you're making a difference, you deserve more than this."

Graveyard Phantom tilted his head in curiosity. "What do you mean?"

Eliza took a deep breath. "I have a spare bedroom in my apartment. It's not much, but it's warm and comfortable. I'd like to offer it to you. It could give you a place to rest and recharge without having to spend every night outside."

Graveyard Phantom was taken aback by the generous offer. "That's very kind of you, Eliza. I appreciate it, but I don't want to impose."

Eliza shook her head. "It's not an imposition. I genuinely want to help you. And besides, it would give us more opportunities to work on ways to improve your public image. We can brainstorm together in a more comfortable setting."

After a moment of consideration, Graveyard Phantom agreed. The idea of having a stable, warm place to stay was appealing, and Eliza's offer was too generous to refuse. They made their way to Eliza's apartment, a modest yet cozy space that reflected her warm personality.

As Graveyard Phantom stepped into the apartment, he marveled at the simple comforts he had never fully experienced before. The soft lighting, the warmth of the indoor heating, and the inviting atmosphere were a stark contrast to the cold park he had grown accustomed to. Eliza led him to the spare bedroom, which had been freshly tidied and furnished with a comfortable bed and a few personal touches that made it feel homey.

Graveyard Phantom took a moment to absorb his new surroundings, feeling a deep sense of gratitude. "This is incredible, Eliza. I can't thank you enough for this."

Eliza smiled, feeling a sense of satisfaction. "I'm glad you like it. You deserve to be comfortable, especially after all the hard work you've put in."

They spent the evening talking, the conversation flowing easily as they shared stories about their lives and dreams. Eliza found herself opening up to Graveyard Phantom in a way she hadn't with many others. His sincerity and commitment had touched her deeply, and she was increasingly drawn to his determination and kindness.

As they sat together in the living room, Eliza's eyes fell on Graveyard Phantom's costume, which he had hung up on a coat rack. She had an idea. "You know, we've made a lot of progress, but I've been thinking about your costume. While it's impressive, it might still be intimidating for some people."

Graveyard Phantom nodded thoughtfully. "I've been trying to balance being seen as a hero while not being overly frightening. What do you have in mind?"

Eliza's face lit up with enthusiasm. "Instead of changing it completely, how about we add some elements that soften its appearance without compromising its essence? We could incorporate some brighter colors or symbols that convey hope and courage."

Graveyard Phantom's eyes gleamed with interest. "That sounds like a good idea. I'd love to hear more about your thoughts on this."

They spent the rest of the night sketching and discussing various modifications to the costume. Eliza's creative ideas included adding a symbol of valor to the chest, incorporating a subtle glow that could be calming rather than eerie, and choosing colors that conveyed warmth and heroism. Graveyard Phantom was impressed by her ingenuity and felt a renewed sense of excitement about the prospect of a revised costume that would better reflect his mission.

As the night wore on, Eliza showed Graveyard Phantom how to operate the television in the living room. Although the screen wasn't as captivating as Eliza's company, he appreciated the gesture. They watched a few shows together, the experience of sharing this simple pleasure with Eliza adding to his growing sense of contentment.

When it was time for bed, Graveyard Phantom settled into the new, comfortable bed in his spare room. The softness of the mattress and the warmth of the blankets were a luxury he had not experienced in centuries. He lay there, reflecting on the incredible changes in his life over the past few weeks.

In the quiet of the night, as he listened to the distant hum of the city and the comforting sounds of Eliza's apartment, Graveyard Phantom felt a profound sense of happiness. For the first time in hundreds of years, he felt truly at ease. The challenges ahead were still uncertain, but with Eliza's support and his new living arrangements, he felt more hopeful and determined than ever before.

The following morning, Graveyard Phantom woke refreshed and eager to begin the day. Eliza had already prepared a hearty breakfast, and they spent the meal discussing their plans for the costume redesign and upcoming community events.

As they worked together, their bond grew stronger, and their affection for each other became increasingly evident. Graveyard Phantom's presence in Eliza's life had brought a new dimension to her days, and she found herself more invested in his success and well-being.

With Eliza's continued support and the improvements to his costume, Graveyard Phantom felt confident that he was on the right path. The city might still have its reservations, but he was determined to prove himself as the hero he aspired to be. And with Eliza by his side, he knew that he had found more than just a place to stay—he had found a friend who believed in him and a chance for a new beginning.

The days turned into weeks, and the bond between Eliza and Graveyard Phantom continued to deepen. They had settled into a comfortable routine, balancing their time between patrolling the city and enjoying each other's company. The initial awkwardness of their living arrangement had dissolved, replaced by an easy companionship that seemed as natural as it was inevitable.

As their affection for each other grew stronger, it became clear that their connection was more than just friendship. Graveyard Phantom had become more than a mere protector in Eliza's eyes—he was a partner, someone she trusted implicitly and whose company she cherished. Likewise, Graveyard Phantom found himself drawn to Eliza in a way he hadn't felt for centuries. Her kindness, her creativity, and her unwavering belief in him had sparked something inside him that he thought had long been lost.

One evening, after another successful patrol, they returned to Eliza's apartment, exhilarated from the night's events. As they sat together on the couch, Graveyard Phantom turned to Eliza, an idea forming in his mind.

"You know, Eliza," he began, his tone thoughtful, "we've been working together so well. You've been by my side through everything, and I couldn't ask for a better partner. I've been thinking... maybe you should have your own superhero costume."

Eliza's eyes widened in surprise and excitement. "My own costume? You really think so?"

Graveyard Phantom nodded enthusiastically. "Absolutely. You're already doing so much—helping with the planning, the strategies, and even being there with me during patrols. You deserve to have a costume that reflects your role in all this. We're a team, after all."

Eliza smiled, her heart fluttering at the idea. "I love that! But what should it look like?"

Graveyard Phantom grinned, leaning forward with a playful glint in his eye. "Well, that's up to you. What do you want it to look like?"

Eliza thought for a moment, considering the possibilities. Her gaze shifted to Graveyard Phantom's costume, which hung in its usual place by the door. She admired its design, the balance it struck between imposing and heroic. Then, a warm smile spread across her face as an idea took root.

"You know," she said softly, "since we're partners, I think I'd like my costume to resemble yours. We could match—like a true team."

Graveyard Phantom's expression softened, touched by her words. "You want it to look like mine?"

Eliza nodded, her voice sincere. "Yes. We're in this together, right? It would mean a lot to me if my costume reflected that. Plus, it would be a reminder that I'm not doing this alone—I've got you by my side."

Graveyard Phantom felt a surge of emotion at her words. Her loyalty and the growing connection between them were more than he ever could have hoped for. "Then it's settled," he said, his voice full of warmth. "We'll design a costume that's just as strong and courageous as you are."

They spent the next few days working on the new costume together. Eliza's creative input was invaluable, and with Graveyard Phantom's expertise, they crafted a suit that mirrored his own in design but with subtle differences that made it uniquely hers. The colors were softer, with a mix of silver and deep blue that complemented Graveyard Phantom's darker palette. The suit had the same sleek lines and protective elements, but it was tailored to Eliza's form, giving it a sense of elegance and power.

As they worked, their connection only grew stronger. Eliza found herself increasingly drawn to Graveyard Phantom , not just as a friend or a partner, but as something more. She began to fantasize about what it would be like if their relationship evolved beyond the boundaries of friendship. The thought of being with him, truly being with him, filled her with a warmth that she hadn't felt in years.

At night, after their work was done, Eliza would lie in bed, her mind drifting to Graveyard Phantom . She imagined what it would be like to share more than just patrols and plans—to share her life with him. The idea of waking up beside him, of facing the world together not just as partners in heroism but as partners in life, was both thrilling and terrifying.

Graveyard Phantom , too, was aware of the growing tension between them. He couldn't ignore the way his heart raced when Eliza was near, or the sense of fulfillment he felt whenever they were together. The thought of her smile, her laugh, and the way she looked at him with such trust and admiration stirred feelings he hadn't experienced in centuries. But he also knew the challenges they faced—he was a being from the Underworld, and she was alive. The differences between them were vast, and yet, the connection they shared seemed to transcend those boundaries.

One night, after they had completed the final touches on Eliza's costume, she stepped back to admire their work. "It's perfect," she said softly, running her fingers over the material. "Thank you, Graveyard Phantom . This means so much to me."

He smiled, his gaze lingering on her. "You've done just as much to make this possible. We're a team, Eliza, and this is just the beginning."

Eliza's heart swelled with affection as she looked into his eyes. "I couldn't have asked for a better partner."

As they stood there, the unspoken feelings between them seemed to hang in the air, waiting to be acknowledged. But neither of them spoke, too uncertain of what might happen if they crossed that line. Instead, they simply enjoyed the moment, content in the knowledge that whatever came next, they would face it together.

With her new costume, Eliza was ready to take on the world by Graveyard Phantom's side. And as they prepared for their next patrol, she couldn't help but wonder what the future held for them—not just as heroes, but as two souls who had found something truly special in each other.

The night awaited, and so did the city, but in that quiet moment in Eliza's apartment, it was just the two of them, their hearts beating in sync as they took the next step in their journey together.

Chapter 3: Dreams of the Road

Graveyard Phantom sat in his room, the soft glow of a bedside lamp illuminating the pages of his favorite comic book. His skeletal fingers traced the bold lines of the illustrations, the colorful panels showcasing the adventures of heroes who roamed the city in sleek, powerful vehicles. As he turned the pages, his mind began to wander, imagining himself and Eliza soaring through the city not just in their costumes, but in something more—something that could match the grandeur of their missions.

He looked up from the comic, his eyes drifting toward the window where the city's lights flickered in the distance. The idea took root in his mind, growing stronger with each passing moment. They had been doing so much good together, but there was always room for improvement, always another level to reach.

The sound of Eliza's soft footsteps broke his reverie. She appeared in the doorway, a smile playing on her lips as she noticed the comic book in his hands. "Still studying those heroes?" she teased lightly, stepping into the room. "What's on your mind, Graveyard Phantom?"

Graveyard Phantom turned to her, his skeletal face unable to show the full range of his excitement, but his voice carried the enthusiasm he felt. "Eliza, I've been thinking... you know how in the comic books, the heroes always have these amazing vehicles? Something that makes their missions even more impressive?"

Eliza chuckled, settling onto the edge of the bed beside him. "You mean like the Car's with gadgets? Or the jet from those other comics? Yeah, I remember. But where would we even begin to build something like that?"

Graveyard Phantom leaned forward, his voice brimming with determination. "There are vehicle salvage yards all around the city. They're full of old, forgotten cars and parts. We could find everything we need to build something incredible—something that would be our own, a vehicle that's just as unique as we are."

Eliza's laughter filled the room, her eyes sparkling with amusement. "You're serious, aren't you?" she said, her tone both surprised and impressed. "You really want to build our own superhero vehicle?"

Graveyard Phantom nodded, the excitement in his voice undeniable. "Think about it, Eliza! With a vehicle like that, we could cover more ground, respond to emergencies faster, and even have a place to regroup during missions. And... well, there's something else."

Eliza tilted her head, curiosity piqued. "What else?"

Graveyard Phantom hesitated for a moment, then continued. "I've been thinking about us, and where we are now. We've been working together so well, and... I think it's time for us to take the next step. We've been staying in this apartment, but it's small, and it doesn't have the space we need to build something like this. There's that two-story house you love—the one with the big garage and the yard. We could afford to move there, build our vehicle, and have plenty of space to make it our own."

Eliza's heart began to race, her pulse quickening at the thought of moving in together, of building something new and exciting with Graveyard Phantom . The idea of them living in a house—a real home—was both thrilling and terrifying. She could feel her heartbeat in her ears, the prospect of sharing a life with him becoming more real with each passing second.

"Are you sure?" she asked, her voice barely above a whisper. "This is a big step, and I... I want to be sure it's what you want too."

Graveyard Phantom reached out, gently taking her hand in his. "Eliza, I've been around for centuries, and in all that time, I've never felt as alive as I do now, with you. I want this—I want to build something amazing with you, to live together, and to keep growing as partners. We can do this, Eliza. Together."

Eliza looked into his eyes, her heart swelling with emotion. She had never expected her life to take this turn, but now that it had, she couldn't imagine anything else. The thought of creating something with Graveyard Phantom —something that would be theirs alone—filled her with a sense of purpose and joy that she hadn't known was possible.

"Let's do it," she said, her voice filled with conviction. "Let's build our superhero vehicle, let's move into that house, and let's make it ours."

Graveyard Phantom's eyes gleamed with excitement. "Then it's settled. Tomorrow, we'll start looking at the salvage yards, and we'll find everything we need to bring this idea to life. And once we have it, we'll be unstoppable."

They spent the rest of the night discussing plans, sketching out ideas for the vehicle and imagining what it could become. They talked about the house too, envisioning what their new life would look like, and with every word, their bond grew stronger.

As the sun began to rise, they finally drifted off to sleep, their minds filled with dreams of the future. The next chapter of their journey was about to begin, and they were ready to face it—together.

Eliza awoke to the soft glow of morning sunlight filtering through the curtains, casting a warm, golden hue across the room. She blinked a few times, the remnants of sleep still clinging to her mind, before she noticed the papers strewn around them. They had fallen asleep in the midst of their plans—sketches of vehicles, notes about the house, and ideas for their future were scattered across the bed and floor.

A smile spread across her face as she remembered the night before. The laughter, the excitement, and the shared dreams had filled her heart with a joy she hadn't known in a long time. She turned to Graveyard Phantom , who lay beside her, still asleep. His skeletal form seemed almost peaceful in the soft morning light, the hard edges softened by the golden glow.

Eliza leaned over, gently placing a hand on his arm. "Good morning, partner," she whispered, her voice soft and filled with affection. A playful grin began to form on her face as she watched him stir, his eyes slowly opening to meet hers.

Graveyard Phantom blinked a few times, disoriented for a moment before he remembered where he was. He looked around at the sketches and notes, then back at Eliza, who was now grinning at him. "Good morning," he replied, his voice still rough with sleep but carrying a note of warmth. "Did we fall asleep mid-mission planning?"

Eliza chuckled, nodding. "Looks like it. We must have been more tired than we realized. But it was worth it—we got so much done. And we had a lot of fun, too."

Graveyard Phantom sat up, stretching his limbs as much as his skeletal form allowed. "I can't remember the last time I had so much fun planning something," he admitted. "You've brought a lot of life back into my existence, Eliza. I'm glad we're doing this together."

Eliza's heart fluttered at his words, and she felt a warmth spread through her chest. There was something about Graveyard Phantom that made her feel like anything was possible, like they could take on the world together. She reached for one of the sketches, holding it up between them. "So, partner, what's the plan for today? Are we heading out to start scavenging for parts?"

Graveyard Phantom nodded, his eyes lighting up with enthusiasm. "Absolutely. We'll visit a few of the salvage yards I know about, see what we can find. With any luck, we'll have the basics for our vehicle by the end of the day."

Eliza grinned, feeling a surge of excitement at the prospect of getting started. "Sounds perfect. And after that, maybe we can swing by that house and take another look? I'm getting more and more excited about the idea of moving in."

Graveyard Phantom's eyes softened as he looked at her, the thought of sharing a home with Eliza filling him with a sense of belonging he hadn't felt in centuries. "I'd like that," he said, his voice gentle. "I think it's going to be the perfect place for us."

They spent the next few minutes tidying up the papers, carefully stacking the sketches and notes on the bedside table. Once the room was in order, Eliza stood up, stretching her arms above her head with a contented sigh. "I'll make us some breakfast," she offered, turning to Graveyard Phantom with a smile. "We'll need our energy for today's adventures."

Graveyard Phantom nodded, standing up beside her. "I'll help. I may not eat much, but I can still enjoy cooking with you."

Eliza's smile widened, and together they headed to the kitchen, their laughter filling the apartment as they prepared for the day ahead. There was something incredibly comforting about their partnership, something that made Eliza feel like they were more than just friends or roommates. As they worked side by side, she couldn't help but imagine what it would be like to wake up like this every morning, in their new home, with Graveyard Phantom by her side.

As they sat down to eat, Eliza looked across the table at him, her heart swelling with affection. She knew that whatever challenges lay ahead, they would face them together. And with every passing moment, she felt herself falling more and more in love with the Skeleton Man who had become her closest friend, her partner, and perhaps, someday, something even more.

Graveyard Phantom and Eliza stood side by side, gazing at the two-story house they had been dreaming about for weeks. It was a charming old place with a wide porch, tall windows, and a sprawling yard that would be perfect for their new life together. The sun was shining brightly overhead, casting a warm glow on the freshly painted exterior. Eliza felt a sense of pride and anticipation bubbling up inside her as they waited for the realtor to arrive.

Graveyard Phantom turned to her, his skeletal face breaking into what she had come to recognize as a smile. "Are you ready for this, Eliza?" he asked, his voice filled with excitement and a hint of nervousness.

Eliza looked up at him, her heart swelling with affection. "More than ready," she replied, squeezing his bony hand. "This is the start of something amazing, and I wouldn't want to do it with anyone else."

Just then, the realtor, a cheerful woman named Mrs. Fields, pulled up in her car. She stepped out, beaming at them as she approached. "Good morning! Are you two excited?" she asked, holding out a set of keys.

Eliza and Graveyard Phantom exchanged a glance before nodding eagerly. "Absolutely," Eliza said, taking the keys from Mrs. Fields. "We've been looking forward to this day for a long time."

Mrs. Fields smiled warmly. "Well, I'm happy to say everything is in order. The house is yours—paid in full. Congratulations on becoming homeowners!"

Graveyard Phantom reached out and took the keys from Eliza, turning them over in his hand as if he could hardly believe it. "Thank you," he said to Mrs. Fields, his voice low with emotion. "This means more to us than you can imagine."

Mrs. Fields nodded, her eyes softening as she looked at the two of them. "I'm sure you'll make this place your own. It's a wonderful house with a lot of history. I can't wait to see what you do with it."

After a few more words, Mrs. Fields bid them farewell, leaving Graveyard Phantom and Eliza standing in front of their new home. They looked at each other, a mix of excitement and nervousness in their eyes.

"Well," Eliza said, holding out her hand, "shall we?"

Graveyard Phantom took her hand, and together they walked up the steps and through the front door, stepping into the future they had both been dreaming of.

Months passed in a blur of activity. During the day, Eliza and Graveyard Phantom scoured the city's salvage yards, searching for the perfect parts to build the car they had designed. The evenings were spent working together in their garage, which was now filled with tools, engine parts, and blueprints. Each piece they added to the vehicle brought them closer to their dream, and with every bolt tightened and every panel welded into place, their bond grew stronger.

The car was taking shape, and it was becoming everything they had envisioned—a beast of a machine with hot, large wheels, a roaring big motor, and the kind of speed that would leave anything else on the road eating dust. It was a labor of love, and as the weeks turned into months, their creation began to come alive.

One evening, as they stood in the garage, looking at the nearly completed vehicle, Graveyard Phantom turned to Eliza, his eyes shining with pride. "We're almost there," he said, his voice filled with awe. "This... this is incredible. We've really done it, Eliza."

Eliza, covered in grease and dirt but smiling from ear to ear, nodded. "It's everything we dreamed of and more. I can't wait to take it for a spin."

Finally, the day came when the last piece was put into place, the final adjustments made. They stood back, admiring their work. The car gleamed under the garage lights, a powerful, sleek machine that looked like it could take on anything.

Graveyard Phantom turned to Eliza, excitement radiating from him. "Are you ready to test it out?"

Eliza grinned, her heart pounding with anticipation. "More than ready. Let's see what this baby can do."

They climbed into the car, the leather seats hugging their bodies as Graveyard Phantom turned the key in the ignition. The engine roared to life, a deep, throaty growl that sent shivers down Eliza's spine. She looked over at Graveyard Phantom , her eyes sparkling with excitement. "Let's do this."

Graveyard Phantom revved the engine, the car vibrating with power, before he eased it out of the garage and onto the street. They drove slowly at first, getting a feel for the vehicle, but as they hit the open road, Graveyard Phantom pressed down on the accelerator, and the car shot forward like a rocket.

The wind whipped through Eliza's hair, and she let out a whoop of joy as they raced down the highway, the world a blur around them. Graveyard Phantom was laughing, a deep, joyous sound that filled the car as they pushed the vehicle to its limits. It was fast, powerful, and everything they had hoped for.

After a while, they slowed down, pulling off to the side of the road and parking the car. They sat there for a moment, catching their breath, the adrenaline still pumping through their veins. Eliza turned to Graveyard Phantom , her heart full of happiness. "That was amazing," she said, her voice breathless. "We really did it."

Graveyard Phantom nodded, his eyes shining as he looked at her. "We did. And this is just the beginning. There's so much more we can do together, Eliza. This is our future."

Eliza reached over and took his hand, her heart swelling with love and anticipation for what was to come. "I know," she said softly. "And I can't wait to see where it takes us."

As they sat there, the sun beginning to set on the horizon, they both knew that this was more than just a car or a house—it was the start of a life they were building together, one filled with adventure, love, and endless possibilities. And as they drove back to their new home, they did so with the knowledge that they were ready for whatever the future held, as long as they faced it together.

Chapter 4: A New Dawn

Graveyard Phantom stood in the garage, surveying their masterpiece—the car gleaming under the overhead lights, a symbol of all the hard work, late nights, and love that had gone into its creation. It had been months of effort, but everything had come together perfectly. And now, with the roar of the engine still echoing in his bones, he felt something he hadn't in centuries: a sense of belonging.

Eliza entered the garage, her eyes sparkling as she took in the sight of Graveyard Phantom standing proudly next to their creation. She had watched him grow more confident and stronger with each passing day, his presence becoming something more than just the ghostly figure she had met in the park. He had become her partner, her friend, and something deeper she was only just beginning to understand.

"Hey," she called out softly, drawing his attention. He turned, and the way he looked at her made her heart skip a beat. There was something in his eyes—a warmth, a depth that hadn't been there before. She felt her own confidence growing, fueled by the bond they had forged.

"Eliza," he said, his voice low and filled with emotion. "We've done so much together... I don't even know where to begin thanking you."

Eliza smiled, walking over to him and placing her hand gently on his arm. "You don't have to thank me, Phantom. This—everything we've done—has been a dream come true for me, too. I've never felt so alive, so... connected."

Graveyard Phantom nodded, his gaze never leaving hers. "Neither have I," he admitted. "I've been alone for so long, drifting through the years, but now... now, I have you. And it's changed everything."

They stood there in the quiet of the garage, the air between them charged with unspoken words and unfulfilled desires. Eliza could feel her heart racing, her thoughts tumbling over themselves as she tried to find the right thing to say. But before she could speak, Graveyard Phantom stepped closer, his skeletal hand gently cupping her cheek.

"Eliza," he whispered, his voice trembling slightly. "There's something I've wanted to tell you for a while now..."

She looked up at him, her breath catching in her throat as she waited, the world around them fading away until there was only the two of them.

"I—" Graveyard Phantom began, but the words seemed to fail him. Instead, he leaned in, closing the distance between them, and before either of them could second-guess it, their lips met in a soft, tentative kiss.

The world seemed to stop as Eliza melted into the kiss, her heart pounding in her chest. Graveyard Phantom's touch was gentle, almost reverent, as if he was afraid she might slip away, but she didn't. She kissed him back, pouring all of her feelings into that moment, letting him know without words just how much he meant to her.

When they finally broke apart, both of them were breathless, their foreheads resting against each other as they tried to steady their racing hearts. Eliza's cheeks were flushed, and she could see the same mix of surprise and joy reflected in Graveyard Phantom's eyes.

"I... I've wanted to do that for so long," Graveyard Phantom confessed, his voice hushed. "But I was afraid. Afraid that you wouldn't feel the same."

Eliza smiled, her fingers tracing the contours of his skeletal face. "I feel exactly the same, Phantom," she whispered. "You've become so much more to me than I ever imagined. I don't want to hide it anymore."

Graveyard Phantom pulled her into his arms, holding her close as if he never wanted to let go. "I don't either," he murmured. "You've given me a reason to live again, Eliza. You've brought me back to life in ways I never thought possible."

They stood there in each other's arms, the silence between them comfortable and filled with unspoken promises. Finally, Eliza pulled back just enough to look into his eyes, her heart fluttering with a mix of anticipation and nerves.

"Phantom," she began, her voice soft and shy, "maybe... maybe we can share the bedroom together tonight?"

Her words hung in the air, and for a moment, Graveyard Phantom seemed taken aback, as if he hadn't expected her to say it. But then, a slow smile spread across his face, and he nodded.

"I would love that," he replied, his voice filled with warmth. "More than anything."

Eliza's heart raced as they walked hand in hand to the bedroom. It was a new beginning for them, a step into something more than just friendship or partnership. It was the start of a deeper connection, one that she had never truly believed she would find—especially not with someone like Graveyard Phantom .

As they entered the room, Eliza felt a sense of calm wash over her, replacing the nervousness she had felt moments before. She knew this was right; she knew that this was where she was meant to be, with him, in this moment.

They spent the night talking, laughing, and sharing stories they had never told anyone else. And when they finally fell asleep in each other's arms, it was with the knowledge that they were no longer alone in the world.

For the first time in his long existence, Graveyard Phantom had found a place where he belonged, and for Eliza, she had found a love that transcended the boundaries of life and death. They were ready to face whatever the future held, together, as partners, as lovers, and as something more than either of them had ever dreamed of.

Morning light filtered through the curtains, casting a soft glow over the bedroom. Eliza stirred, slowly waking to the warmth of Graveyard Phantom's embrace. The events of the previous night replayed in her mind, and a contented smile spread across her face. For the first time in years, she felt complete—like all the pieces of her life had finally fallen into place.

Graveyard Phantom , too, was awake, his eyes watching her with a tenderness that made her heart flutter. As their gazes met, the reality of their situation began to settle in. They had crossed a line, stepping into a new chapter of their relationship, one filled with love and commitment. But with this new beginning came a host of complicated questions, ones that neither of them could ignore.

Eliza shifted slightly, propping herself up on her elbow as she looked at Graveyard Phantom . "There's something we need to talk about," she said softly, her voice tinged with uncertainty. "You're from the Underworld, and I'm still... well, alive. What does that mean for us?"

Graveyard Phantom's expression grew serious as he considered her words. He had thought about this too, in the quiet moments when he wasn't by her side. It was a question that had no easy answer, and yet, he knew they had to face it together.

"Eliza," he began, his voice steady but gentle, "I've lived for centuries, drifting between the world of the living and the Underworld. I've seen things change, people come and go, but I've never felt connected to anyone the way I do with you. I don't want to lose that, lose you."

Eliza reached out, taking his hand in hers. "But what does that mean for us?" she asked again, her eyes searching his. "I can't stay young forever. Eventually, I'll grow old, and one day, I'll pass away. What happens then?"

Graveyard Phantom squeezed her hand, his skeletal fingers surprisingly warm against her skin. "We'll live the rest of your life together," he said, his voice filled with conviction. "We'll cherish every moment, every day, until your time comes. And when it does, Eliza, I promise you this: we'll be together forever in the Land of the Living Dead."

His words hung in the air, and Eliza felt a mixture of emotions swirling inside her—relief, sadness, and a deep sense of love. The idea of spending her life with Graveyard Phantom , knowing that even death wouldn't separate them, brought her comfort. But it also reminded her of the inevitable passage of time, something she had never truly grappled with until now.

"Are you sure?" she asked, her voice barely above a whisper. "I don't want to hold you back from your world, from what you were before."

Graveyard Phantom smiled, a warmth in his eyes that she had come to adore. "I've already lived for so long, Eliza, without purpose, without love. Meeting you, being with you—it's given me a reason to exist, a reason to fight for something more. The Underworld will still be there when the time comes, but I want to spend as much of this life with you as I can."

Eliza felt tears welling up in her eyes, but they were tears of happiness, of gratitude for the love they had found in each other. She leaned in, kissing him softly, pouring all of her emotions into that one simple act.

"Then that's what we'll do," she whispered against his lips. "We'll make the most of every moment we have, together."

Graveyard Phantom pulled her closer, holding her as if he never wanted to let go. "I love you, Eliza," he said, the words filled with a depth of feeling that only centuries of loneliness could create.

"I love you too," Eliza replied, her heart full to bursting.

For the rest of the morning, they stayed in bed, wrapped in each other's arms, talking about the future. They made plans for the house they had bought together, imagining a life filled with laughter, love, and adventure. They discussed the possibility of building a new life together, where Graveyard Phantom could continue his role as a superhero, with Eliza by his side as his partner.

And as they talked, the questions and uncertainties that had once seemed so daunting began to fade away. They realized that they didn't need all the answers right now. What mattered was that they had each other, and together, they could face whatever challenges the future might bring.

As the day wore on, they finally got out of bed, ready to begin this new chapter of their lives. There was so much to do, so many dreams to chase, and they were eager to get started. But no matter what the future held, they knew one thing for certain: they would face it together, as partners, as lovers, and as something more—two souls bound by love, destined to be together, in this life and beyond.

The days that followed were filled with a whirlwind of activity, as Eliza and Graveyard Phantom settled into their new life together. The house they had purchased, nestled in a quiet neighborhood with a view of the city skyline, quickly became their sanctuary—a place where they could escape from the world and just be themselves.

Graveyard Phantom , despite being a centuries-old being from the Underworld, took to domestic life with surprising ease. He enjoyed the routine of their days: waking up together, sharing meals, and working on various projects around the house. But what he loved most was spending time with Eliza, their conversations ranging from the mundane to the profound, always deepening their connection.

One evening, as the sun dipped below the horizon and the city lights began to twinkle, Graveyard Phantom found himself standing in the garage, gazing at the nearly completed car they had been building together. It was a beast of a machine, with hot, large wheels, a big motor, and the kind of sleek design that made it look like it could outrun anything on the road. It was their dream creation, a testament to their partnership and shared passion.

Eliza walked in, wiping her hands on a rag, a satisfied smile on her face. "It's almost ready," she said, admiring the car. "I can't believe we actually did it."

Graveyard Phantom turned to her, his eyes reflecting the soft glow of the overhead lights. "We make a pretty good team," he said, a hint of pride in his voice.

Eliza nodded, leaning against the car and crossing her arms. "Yeah, we do." She paused, looking at him thoughtfully. "You know, I've been thinking a lot about us...about everything."

Graveyard Phantom moved closer, sensing the seriousness in her tone. "What's on your mind?" he asked, his voice gentle.

Eliza hesitated for a moment, then took a deep breath. "I know we've talked about the future, about what happens when...when my time comes," she began, her eyes searching his face. "But there's something else I need to know. Are you truly happy here? I mean, you've lived for so long, seen so much...is this enough for you?"

Graveyard Phantom reached out, taking her hands in his. "Eliza," he said softly, "I've never been happier in my entire existence. You've given me something I never thought I'd have again—purpose, love, a reason to wake up every day. This life we've started building together...it's everything I could have ever hoped for."

Eliza smiled, relief washing over her. "I'm glad to hear that," she said, her voice tinged with emotion. "Because I want this too, more than anything. But sometimes I worry that I'm holding you back, keeping you from something greater."

Graveyard Phantom shook his head, his grip on her hands tightening. "You're not holding me back. You're the reason I've come this far. Without you, I wouldn't have the strength to do any of this. And as for something greater...there's nothing greater than being with you."

Eliza felt tears prick at the corners of her eyes, but she blinked them away, not wanting to lose this moment. "Then let's keep building this life together," she said, her voice firm. "Let's make every day count."

Graveyard Phantom leaned in, pressing a soft kiss to her forehead. "We will," he promised. "We'll face whatever comes our way, together."

The following weeks were a blur of activity as they finalized the car and made the house truly their own. Graveyard Phantom grew more confident, not just in his role as a superhero, but in his new life with Eliza. They continued to train together, honing their skills and preparing for whatever challenges might come their way.

But it wasn't just about the work. Their affection for each other grew stronger with each passing day, and the bond between them deepened in ways they hadn't expected. They spent their evenings curled up on the couch, watching old movies or simply talking about their hopes and dreams. And every night, as they lay in bed together, Eliza would fall asleep with a smile on her face, knowing that she was right where she was meant to be.

One night, after a particularly successful training session, they stood together in the living room, gazing out at the city lights. Graveyard Phantom wrapped his arm around Eliza's shoulders, pulling her close.

"You know," Eliza said, her voice soft, "I think we make a pretty amazing team."

Graveyard Phantom smiled, pressing a kiss to the top of her head. "We do," he agreed. "And this is just the beginning."

As they stood there, the weight of their love and commitment settled over them, wrapping them in a warmth that neither of them had ever known before. They were ready for whatever the future held, knowing that they would face it together, as partners, as lovers, and as something more.

And in that moment, with the city spread out before them and the promise of endless possibilities on the horizon, they knew that their new beginning was just the start of an incredible journey—one that they would walk together, hand in hand, for the rest of their days.

Chapter 5: The Weight of the Future

Graveyard Phantom sat on the edge of their bed, lost in thought. The room was dimly lit by the soft glow of the moon filtering through the curtains. His gaze was fixed on the floor, but his mind was far away, tangled in a web of questions and uncertainties. He had never expected to find himself here—in a home, with someone he loved more than anything in the world. And yet, as much as he cherished every moment with Eliza, there was a lingering doubt that gnawed at him, a fear that he couldn't shake.

He heard the soft sound of footsteps approaching and looked up as Eliza entered the bedroom. She was wearing one of his oversized shirts, her hair loosely tied back, her face glowing with the warmth and comfort of home. She smiled at him as she crossed the room, but her smile faltered when she noticed the look on his face.

"Phantom," she said softly, sitting down beside him. "What's on your mind?"

Graveyard Phantom hesitated, searching for the right words. He didn't want to burden her with his fears, but he knew he couldn't keep them bottled up any longer. He took a deep breath, then spoke in a voice barely above a whisper.

"Eliza...are you truly happy?" he asked, his eyes meeting hers. "Am I holding you back from enjoying the life of the living?"

Eliza's brow furrowed in concern as she looked at him, trying to understand the depth of his worry. "What do you mean?" she asked gently.

Graveyard Phantom sighed, running a hand through his hair. "I mean...what about everything you've always dreamed of? A life filled with the things you've imagined—children, a future that's...normal. I'm not sure if we could have children, Eliza. And I'm not like other men. I'm not even...alive, not really."

Eliza's heart ached at the vulnerability in his voice, at the way he seemed to be questioning his place in her life. She reached out, taking his hand in hers, and squeezed it reassuringly.

"Phantom, listen to me," she said, her voice steady and filled with love. "Yes, I'm happy. I've never been happier in my entire life. And you're not holding me back from anything. You've brought so much joy and meaning into my life—things I never knew I was missing until I met you."

Graveyard Phantom looked at her, his expression softening as he listened to her words. But the doubt still lingered in his mind, and he couldn't help but ask, "But what about children, Eliza? What if we can't...what if we can't have them?"

Eliza paused, thinking carefully about her response. It was a question that had crossed her mind as well, but she had never allowed it to overshadow the love she felt for him. She knew that their relationship was unique, unlike anything she had ever imagined, and she was willing to face whatever challenges came their way.

"Phantom," she began, choosing her words with care, "I don't know what the future holds for us. Maybe we'll have children, maybe we won't. But what I do know is that I want to face that future with you. Whatever happens, we'll figure it out together. And that's enough for me."

She leaned closer, her hand reaching up to cup his cheek, her thumb gently brushing against his boney cheek. "Yes, I'm sure," she continued, her voice filled with certainty. "And let's see what the future has for us as we grow together. I wouldn't want to spend it with anyone else but you."

Graveyard Phantom felt a surge of emotion welling up inside him as he listened to her. He had spent so many years alone, wandering the Underworld, convinced that love and happiness were beyond his reach. But now, here she was—this incredible woman who had not only accepted him for who he was but had also embraced the life they were building together. The weight of his doubts and fears began to lift, replaced by a deep sense of gratitude and love.

Without another word, he pulled Eliza into a gentle hug, holding her close as he buried his face in her hair. "Thank you," he whispered, his voice thick with emotion. "Thank you for everything."

Eliza wrapped her arms around him, resting her head against his chest. She could feel the steady beat of his heart, a reminder that despite everything, he was real—he was hers. They stayed like that for a long time, wrapped in each other's embrace, the world outside their window fading away.

As they held each other, Graveyard Phantom realized that he had been given a second chance at life—a life filled with love, hope, and endless possibilities. And as long as he had Eliza by his side, he knew that they could face anything the future might bring.

When they finally pulled away, Eliza looked up at him with a soft smile. "Come on," she said, taking his hand and leading him towards the bed. "Let's get some rest. We have a lot of adventures ahead of us."

Graveyard Phantom smiled, his heart lighter than it had been in centuries. He nodded, following her lead as they climbed into bed together. As they settled under the covers, Eliza nestled close to him, her head resting on his shoulder.

And as the night wore on, with the moon casting its gentle light over them, Graveyard Phantom knew that he had found something truly extraordinary—a love that transcended life and death, a bond that would endure for all eternity.

As the days turned into weeks, and the weeks into months, Graveyard Phantom and Eliza's bond only grew stronger. The love they shared was something rare and beautiful, a connection that defied the very boundaries of life and death. They built a life together, one filled with laughter, warmth, and an unspoken understanding that they were meant to be with one another.

Graveyard Phantom often found himself reflecting on how much his life had changed since that fateful day when he first decided to return to the world of the living. He had come back with the dream of becoming a superhero, a figure of justice and hope for the people of the city. But what he hadn't expected was to find a love so deep, so consuming, that it would transform him in ways he never thought possible.

One evening, as he stood on the rooftop of their new home, gazing out at the city skyline, Graveyard Phantom's thoughts began to drift. The night was cool and quiet, the stars twinkling above like tiny diamonds scattered across the sky. He could hear the faint hum of the city below, the sound of life continuing on, as it always did.

But in this moment, his mind was elsewhere—focused on the future, on the life he and Eliza were building together. He knew that his return to the living world had been nothing short of a miracle, a second chance at life. And he was determined not to waste it.

He clenched his fists, a renewed sense of purpose filling his heart. "My second chance at life, and I'm not going to waste it," he whispered to himself, the words carrying a weight that only he could understand.

Graveyard Phantom had always been driven by a sense of duty, a desire to protect those who could not protect themselves. But now, that drive was fueled by something more—by the love he had for Eliza, by the life they were creating together. He would become the greatest superhero the world had ever known, not just for himself, but for her. He would be the man she deserved, the man she could be proud of.

And more than that, he would be the greatest husband of all time. He would cherish Eliza, love her with all his heart, and stand by her side no matter what challenges they might face. He had been given a gift—an opportunity to experience a love that transcended the very fabric of life itself—and he wasn't going to let anything come between them.

As he stood there, lost in thought, the sound of soft footsteps behind him brought him back to the present. He turned to see Eliza standing in the doorway, her silhouette framed by the warm light of their home. She was wearing a simple dress, her hair loose and flowing around her shoulders. There was a soft smile on her lips as she walked over to him, her presence a comforting balm to his restless mind.

"What are you doing up here all by yourself?" she asked, her voice gentle as she slipped her hand into his.

Graveyard Phantom smiled down at her, his heart swelling with love. "Just thinking," he replied, his thumb brushing over the back of her hand. "About us...about the future."

Eliza tilted her head slightly, her eyes searching his. "And what do you see when you think about the future?" she asked, her voice curious.

Graveyard Phantom took a deep breath, his gaze shifting back to the cityscape. "I see a life filled with love, with adventure. I see us growing old together, building a family...maybe even raising a child or two." He paused, his voice softening. "I see myself becoming the greatest superhero of all time, but more importantly, I see myself becoming the greatest husband...and God willing, the greatest father of all time."

Eliza's heart skipped a beat at his words. She had always known that Graveyard Phantom was driven, that he had a deep sense of duty and responsibility. But hearing him speak so openly about their future, about the life he wanted to build with her, filled her with a warmth that spread through her entire being.

She stepped closer, wrapping her arms around him and resting her head against his chest. "I see that too," she whispered, her voice barely audible. "And I believe in you. You're already the greatest man I've ever known, and I have no doubt that you'll be the greatest husband and father too."

Graveyard Phantom's arms tightened around her, holding her close as if he never wanted to let go. "Thank you," he murmured, his lips brushing against the top of her head. "For believing in me, for standing by my side. I don't know what I did to deserve you, but I'm going to spend the rest of my life proving that I'm worthy of your love."

Eliza looked up at him, her eyes shining with unshed tears. "You don't have to prove anything," she said softly. "You already are."

They stood there together, wrapped in each other's arms, the world around them fading away. In that moment, it didn't matter that Graveyard Phantom had once been a denizen of the Underworld, or that their love defied the natural order of life and death. All that mattered was that they had found each other, and that they were ready to face whatever the future might hold—together.

As the night deepened and the stars continued to shine above, Graveyard Phantom made a silent vow to himself. He would protect this love, nurture it, and let it guide him as he forged his path as a hero, a husband, and one day, perhaps, a father. This was his second chance at life, and with Eliza by his side, he knew that anything was possible.

Graveyard Phantom's mind raced with possibilities as he stood on the rooftop, holding Eliza close. The future they envisioned was within reach, but there were still questions he needed answers to—questions only someone with ancient knowledge could provide.

He knew just the person to consult. "I can talk to the Head Bookman, Mr. Skeletoleyes," Graveyard Phantom said suddenly, pulling back to look into Eliza's eyes. "He has books that are millions of years old. If anyone knows what I can do, it's him."

Eliza's brow furrowed slightly, a mix of curiosity and concern in her gaze. "Mr. Skeletoleyes? I've never heard of him."

Graveyard Phantom smiled reassuringly. "He's the keeper of all knowledge in the Land of the Living Dead. His library is vast, filled with books that contain the wisdom of ages. If there's a way for us to be joined in marriage and for me to become a father, he'll know it."

Eliza nodded, her trust in him unwavering. "Then you should go. Find the answers we need."

With a soft kiss on her forehead, Graveyard Phantom turned and leaped from the rooftop, his spectral form soaring through the night sky as he made his way back to the Land of the Living Dead. The familiar chill of the Underworld welcomed him as he descended into the realm he once called home.

The journey to Mr. Skeletoleyes's library was a daunting one, as the ancient scholar lived in a towering structure made entirely of books—books stacked so high they seemed to touch the very heavens of the Underworld. Graveyard Phantom had to climb the tall staircase, each step creaking under the weight of countless tomes filled with the knowledge of forgotten eras.

Finally, he reached the top, where Mr. Skeletoleyes awaited him. The old skeleton was perched atop a throne made of ancient manuscripts, his bony hands resting on an open book as he peered down at Graveyard Phantom with hollow, glowing eye sockets.

"Skeleton Man... oh, sorry, Graveyard Phantom ," Mr. Skeletoleyes corrected himself with a chuckle. "After hundreds of years calling you Skeleton Man, it's going to take some time to get your new name right."

Graveyard Phantom grinned, though the nerves still fluttered in his chest. "It's alright, Mr. Skeletoleyes. I need your help. I've been given a second chance at life, and I want to make the most of it. But I don't know how. How can Eliza and I be joined in marriage? And... is it even possible for us to have children?"

Mr. Skeletoleyes tapped his chin thoughtfully, his eye sockets narrowing in contemplation. "Ah, love. It's a rare thing, especially for those of us from the Underworld. But it's not impossible." He closed the book he had been reading and set it aside, standing up with a creak of ancient bones. "Give me time to consult the books. The answers you seek are buried deep within the pages of the oldest texts. When I find them, I will send Mr. Crow to fetch you."

Graveyard Phantom nodded, his heart filled with hope. "Thank you, Mr. Skeletoleyes. I'll wait for your message."

With that, Graveyard Phantom descended the towering staircase, the weight of anticipation heavy on his shoulders. He knew it might take time for Mr. Skeletoleyes to find the answers, but he was willing to wait. For Eliza, he would wait an eternity.

As he made his way back to the Land of the Living, his thoughts were filled with possibilities. What if there was a way for them to be together, truly together, in every sense of the word? What if there was a way for him to experience the joys of fatherhood, to raise a child with Eliza by his side?

Graveyard Phantom's heart swelled with determination. He had been given a second chance at life, and he was going to make sure that every moment counted. He would become the greatest superhero, the greatest husband, and, if fate allowed, the greatest father. For now, he would return to Eliza, knowing that whatever the future held, they would face it together—hand in hand, heart to heart.

When Graveyard Phantom returned to their home, Eliza was waiting for him, her eyes lighting up as soon as she saw him. "Did you find what you were looking for?" she asked, concern and hope mingling in her voice.

"Not yet," Graveyard Phantom replied, taking her hand in his. "But Mr. Skeletoleyes is searching for the answers. We'll know soon enough."

Eliza smiled, her faith in him unwavering. "Whatever happens, we'll face it together. I love you, Graveyard Phantom . Nothing will change that."

Graveyard Phantom pulled her into a gentle embrace, his heart full of gratitude. "I love you too, Eliza. And I promise, we'll find a way to make our future everything we've dreamed of."

With those words, the two of them stood together, ready to face whatever challenges lay ahead. They had each other, and that was all they needed to take on the world—living or dead.

Chapter 6: The Message

The sun had just begun to dip below the horizon when Graveyard Phantom stood on a rooftop, watching the twilight sky with a sense of anticipation. The days had passed in a blur of activity, and now Mr. Crow's arrival was imminent. The ancient crow, a trusted messenger of Mr. Skeletoleyes, was known for his reliability and swift deliveries.

As Graveyard Phantom's keen eyes spotted the familiar figure of Mr. Crow against the fading light, his heart quickened. "It's Mr. Crow!" he exclaimed with excitement. "Mr. Skeletoleyes must be sending me a message."

Eliza, who had been standing beside him, looked up with hopeful eyes. "Is this the moment we've been waiting for?"

Graveyard Phantom nodded, his gaze fixed on the approaching crow. Mr. Crow was a majestic creature, his feathers a mix of iridescent black and deep shades of gray. As he landed gracefully on the rooftop, a small scroll was tied to his ankle with a delicate ribbon.

Graveyard Phantom gently retrieved the note, untying it with careful fingers. "Thank you for bringing this, Mr. Crow," he said, offering the bird a small, tasty treat he had prepared. The crow pecked at the treat eagerly before flapping his wings and returning to the underworld, his mission complete.

Eliza watched with bated breath as Graveyard Phantom read the note. The words were written in the elegant, flowing script of Mr. Skeletoleyes, filled with the wisdom and knowledge of the ancient books.

Graveyard Phantom's eyes widened as he scanned the message. "Eliza, this is incredible. Mr. Skeletoleyes has found something important."

He turned to Eliza with a mixture of excitement and urgency. "I need to return to the Underworld. Mr. Skeletoleyes has discovered something that could change everything for us."

Eliza's face showed a mixture of pride and concern. "Be careful, Graveyard Phantom . I'll be waiting for you."

With a determined nod, Graveyard Phantom took to the skies, soaring through the twilight toward the Land of the Living Dead. The journey back was swift, guided by the familiar landmarks of the Underworld. He landed gracefully at the entrance to the towering library, where Mr. Skeletoleyes awaited him.

Mr. Skeletoleyes stood at the top of the grand staircase, his skeletal figure silhouetted against the backdrop of ancient books. "Ah, Graveyard Phantom , you've returned swiftly. I have been studying the texts and have found some remarkable information."

Graveyard Phantom ascended the stairs, his heart pounding with anticipation. "What did you find, Mr. Skeletoleyes? Can we be joined in marriage? Is it possible for us to have children?"

Mr. Skeletoleyes beckoned him to a large, dusty tome laid open on a pedestal. "These texts hold the answers to your questions. The key to your desires lies in the old rituals and ancient practices that were once part of the Underworld's magic."

Graveyard Phantom leaned closer, eager to absorb every detail. "What do I need to do?"

"The rituals are complex," Mr. Skeletoleyes explained, his bony fingers tracing the faded script. "For you and Eliza to be joined in marriage in both worlds, you must perform a binding ceremony that merges both the essence of the living and the dead. As for children, it is a rare and extraordinary possibility, but it requires a special enchantment that intertwines your essence with that of the living."

Graveyard Phantom's eyes lit up with hope. "Tell me what I need to do."

"You must undertake a journey to the Heart of the Underworld," Mr. Skeletoleyes instructed. "There, you will perform the binding ceremony. For the enchantment to work, you'll need to bring a token of your love—a symbol of your commitment and the promise of a future together."

Graveyard Phantom nodded resolutely. "I'll do whatever it takes. Thank you, Mr. Skeletoleyes."

Mr. Skeletoleyes smiled faintly, his skeletal face showing a rare sign of warmth. "I will prepare the necessary texts and rituals for your return. Be mindful of the journey ahead."

With the weight of the knowledge settled firmly in his mind, Graveyard Phantom flew back to the Land of the Living, his thoughts filled with plans and preparations. He could almost see the future unfolding before him—a future where he and Eliza would be together, not just in love but in a life full of possibilities.

As he landed beside Eliza, who had been anxiously waiting for his return, he took her hands in his. "Eliza, Mr. Skeletoleyes has found the answers. We need to perform a special ceremony in the Heart of the Underworld, and we'll need a token of our love."

Eliza's eyes sparkled with excitement. "We'll do it together. I believe in us."

Graveyard Phantom pulled her close, his heart swelling with love and determination. "We'll make our dreams come true, Eliza. This is just the beginning."

With renewed hope and a clear path before them, the couple prepared for the next chapter in their extraordinary journey—one that would bring them closer to realizing their dreams of a life filled with love, adventure, and the promise of a future beyond the boundaries of life and death.

Graveyard Phantom and Eliza stood before the towering figure of Mr. Skeletoleyes, the grand library of the Underworld a silent witness to their pivotal moment. Mr. Skeletoleyes, surrounded by ancient tomes and mystical artifacts, greeted them with a solemn nod.

"Mr. Scott, you've returned," Mr. Skeletoleyes said, his voice echoing with the weight of centuries.

"Mr. Scott?" Graveyard Phantom echoed, confusion flickering across his skeletal features. "Why did you call me Scott?"

Mr. Skeletoleyes' eye sockets glowed faintly as he adjusted his glasses, his voice taking on a nostalgic tone. "That was your name before you became Graveyard Phantom . Joseph Scott. You passed away at the age of 29, a tragic accident involving a wagon. The horse didn't stop in time... what a shame." He shut a massive book with a cloud of dust, his skeletal hand resting atop it. "Now, if you wish to regain your full humanity, you must undertake the journey to the Heart of the Underworld. There, you will complete the necessary rituals."

Graveyard Phantom's eyes widened in disbelief and a mix of awe. "So, you're saying I can return to the Land of the Living, looking as I did when I was 29?"

Mr. Skeletoleyes nodded gravely. "Yes, and with that, you will have the opportunity to become a father. However, remember that once you undertake this transformation, you will face a second passing away event when you grow older. Until then, you cannot return to the Underworld. You will be fully alive and healthy."

Eliza, standing close by, reached out and squeezed Graveyard Phantom's hand. "We're ready for this, Mr. Skeletoleyes. We'll face whatever comes."

"Good," Mr. Skeletoleyes said with a rare flicker of approval. "Once you complete the rituals and your journey to the Heart of the Underworld, we will be able to start the rites for your full transformation. Until then, you must prepare and gather the necessary items for the ritual."

He handed Graveyard Phantom a scroll filled with arcane symbols and instructions. "This text will guide you on your journey. Follow it precisely. When you return, we will begin the rituals to complete your transformation."

Graveyard Phantom took the scroll with a sense of determination. "Thank you, Mr. Skeletoleyes. We won't let you down."

"Indeed," Mr. Skeletoleyes said, his skeletal form becoming slightly more animated. "Remember, this journey will test your resolve and commitment. But if your love is true, you will succeed."

Eliza and Graveyard Phantom exchanged a resolute glance. "We'll do it," Eliza said, her voice steady. "We're in this together."

With that, they bid farewell to Mr. Skeletoleyes and made their way to the entrance of the Underworld. The journey to the Heart of the Underworld was both a physical and emotional endeavor, fraught with trials and challenges that tested their bond and resolve.

As they ventured deeper into the shadowy realms, the path grew darker and more treacherous. The Heart of the Underworld was a place of immense power and ancient magic, guarded by enigmatic forces and eerie phenomena. Graveyard Phantom and Eliza navigated through the labyrinthine passages, their path illuminated only by the faint glow of enchanted lanterns.

Along the way, they encountered spectral beings and faced tests that challenged their courage and unity. Each trial seemed designed to push them to their limits, but their determination and love for each other provided the strength to persevere.

Finally, they reached the Heart of the Underworld—a majestic, otherworldly chamber filled with a pulsating energy. The air crackled with ancient magic, and a grand altar stood at its center, adorned with symbols and relics of bygone eras.

Graveyard Phantom and Eliza approached the altar, their hearts pounding with anticipation. The scroll provided specific instructions for the ritual, and they began the intricate process, carefully following each step.

As the ritual progressed, the chamber was bathed in a shimmering light, and a powerful surge of magic enveloped them. Graveyard Phantom felt a profound shift within himself, a melding of his former life and his current existence. The transformation process was both exhilarating and overwhelming, a testament to the strength of their love and their shared resolve.

When the ritual was complete, the Heart of the Underworld began to settle, its energy returning to a calm state. Graveyard Phantom and Eliza, their hands still clasped together, felt a deep sense of accomplishment and hope.

"We did it," Graveyard Phantom said, his voice filled with awe. "We completed the ritual."

Eliza smiled, her eyes shining with pride and love. "We did. And now we can begin the next chapter of our lives."

With their hearts full of hope and their spirits united, Graveyard Phantom and Eliza made their way back to the Land of the Living. The journey had changed them, strengthening their bond and affirming their commitment to each other.

As they emerged into the familiar world of the living, they knew that their future was now filled with possibilities. The journey ahead would be filled with new challenges and adventures, but they were ready to face them together, with love and determination guiding their way.

The next steps were clear. They would begin the process of integrating their new life, preparing for the future they had always dreamed of. And as they walked hand in hand, they knew that their love would be the foundation upon which they would build their extraordinary future.

As the ancient energies of the Heart of the Underworld settled around them, Graveyard Phantom and Eliza stood side by side, their hands intertwined. The sense of accomplishment was palpable, but the journey had only just begun. Graveyard Phantom turned to Eliza, his gaze tender and reflective.

"Joseph Scott would be a great husband and father," he said softly, the weight of his former identity and his new existence mingling in his voice. "Graveyard Phantom can be the superhero. But tonight, I want it to be just me and you."

Eliza looked into his eyes, her heart swelling with affection and understanding. "Joseph Scott or Graveyard Phantom , you're still the same person I fell in love with. And tonight, it's about us—about our love and the life we're building together."

With the ritual complete, Graveyard Phantom felt a profound sense of relief and hope. He had embraced his past and his future, and now, as Joseph Scott, he could look forward to the life he had always dreamed of—a life with Eliza.

The evening unfolded in a serene and intimate atmosphere. The new home they had created together, with its warm and inviting spaces, felt like a sanctuary from the world. The house, filled with the soft glow of evening light and the gentle hum of their new life, was a testament to their journey and their dreams.

In the cozy living room, Eliza and Graveyard Phantom sat close together, their proximity reflecting the deep connection they shared. The fire crackled softly in the hearth, casting a warm glow across their faces. The room was filled with the comforting scent of lavender and cinnamon, and the ambiance was peaceful and inviting.

Graveyard Phantom looked at Eliza with a mix of gratitude and longing. "I want you to know how much this means to me," he said, his voice gentle. "Tonight is special because it's a celebration of us—our love, our future. It's a chance for us to just be together, without any distractions."

Eliza's eyes sparkled with warmth. "I couldn't agree more. This is our moment, our time to cherish each other and everything we've built together."

They leaned in closer, their foreheads touching as they shared a tender kiss. The kiss was soft and loving, a reflection of the deep bond that had grown between them. It was a moment of pure connection, where their hearts and souls seemed to merge into one.

As they pulled back slightly, their faces illuminated by the soft light of the fire, Eliza took a deep breath and smiled. "Tonight, let's focus on each other. Let's dream about our future and what's to come. We've worked so hard to get here, and now it's time to enjoy the fruits of our labor."

Graveyard Phantom nodded, his eyes filled with affection. "Yes, let's enjoy this moment. And as we look forward to the future, know that I am here for you, as Joseph Scott, as Graveyard Phantom , and as the person who loves you with all my heart."

They spent the evening talking about their dreams and aspirations, their hopes for the future, and the life they envisioned together. The conversation flowed easily, filled with laughter and shared memories. It was a time of deep connection and understanding, where their love for each other was the center of their world.

As the night drew to a close, they retired to their bedroom, their hearts full of love and anticipation. The new bed, a symbol of their fresh start, was a testament to their commitment to each other. They settled in, their bodies close, their hearts beating in unison.

Eliza looked up at Graveyard Phantom , her eyes reflecting the depth of her feelings. "We've come so far, and I'm grateful for every moment. Here's to a future filled with love and happiness."

Graveyard Phantom smiled, his heart full. "To our future, Eliza. To a life together that's full of joy and adventure."

As they held each other close, the world outside seemed to fade away. In that quiet, intimate moment, they found solace and hope in each other. The journey ahead was uncertain, but with their love as their guide, they knew they could face anything together.

In the warmth of their new home and the glow of their shared dreams, Eliza and Graveyard Phantom embraced the new beginning they had created. The night was a celebration of their love, their commitment, and the extraordinary future they were building together.

Chapter 7: A New Dawn

Joseph Scott and Eliza Billings stood hand in hand at the heart of their new home, their lives forever changed. The house, filled with warmth and promise, seemed to pulse with the excitement of their new beginning. Each room was a testament to their journey, reflecting the love and effort they had poured into creating a life together.

The morning sun streamed through the windows, casting a golden glow over their surroundings. Joseph, now fully embracing his second chance at life, felt a profound sense of renewal. His transformation from the Graveyard Phantom of the Underworld to Joseph Scott of the Living World was complete, and with it came the realization of a dream he had long cherished.

Eliza, radiant and full of life, looked at Joseph with a mix of admiration and affection. Their relationship had grown deeper with each passing day, and they were more in love than ever. The thought of a shared future filled her with joy, and the hints of something more significant lingered in the air.

They had spent the past few weeks settling into their new home, each day an adventure of its own. From organizing their belongings to exploring their neighborhood, every moment was a discovery of their new life together. They reveled in the simple pleasures of their routine, finding comfort in the familiarity of each other's presence.

One afternoon, as they relaxed in their living room, Joseph turned to Eliza with a thoughtful expression. "Eliza," he began, his voice soft and earnest, "I've been thinking about our future—about the life we're building together."

Eliza looked up from the book she had been reading, her eyes sparkling with curiosity. "What's on your mind?"

Joseph took a deep breath, his heart pounding with both excitement and nervousness. "This is our chance to start anew, to create a life filled with love and happiness. And I want to make the most of it. There's something important I need to ask you."

Eliza's pulse quickened, a mixture of anticipation and hope swirling within her. "What is it?"

Joseph reached into his pocket and pulled out a small, elegant box. He opened it to reveal a delicate ring, its simplicity and beauty reflecting the depth of his feelings. "Eliza Billings, will you marry me? Will you spend the rest of your life with me, sharing all the joys and challenges that come our way?"

Eliza's eyes welled with tears of happiness as she gazed at the ring and then at Joseph. The weight of his words and the significance of the moment overwhelmed her. "Joseph, this is beautiful," she said softly, her voice filled with emotion. "Of course, I will. I want to spend the rest of my life with you."

With a joyful smile, Joseph slipped the ring onto Eliza's finger. It fit perfectly, symbolizing their commitment and the beginning of a new chapter in their lives. They embraced, their hearts swelling with love and anticipation for the future.

As they held each other close, Joseph and Eliza shared a quiet moment of reflection. The house around them seemed to come alive with the promise of their future together. They spoke of their dreams and plans, of the life they hoped to build, and of the adventures they would undertake as partners.

The days that followed were filled with preparations for their upcoming wedding. They worked together to plan the ceremony, choosing details that reflected their unique journey and their deep connection. Each choice, from the venue to the decorations, was a reflection of their love and the life they were creating.

Their engagement was a time of celebration and joy, a period where their love was reaffirmed and their future was embraced with open hearts. Friends and family gathered to share in their happiness, offering support and well-wishes for the new couple.

As the wedding day approached, Joseph and Eliza continued to build their life together with optimism and enthusiasm. The house, now a symbol of their love and commitment, was transformed into a haven of warmth and happiness. They looked forward to their wedding with excitement, eager to start their life as a married couple.

The future was bright with possibilities, and Joseph Scott was ready to embrace it fully. His second chance at life had given him the opportunity to build something extraordinary with Eliza. Together, they were embarking on a new journey, filled with hope, love, and the promise of a beautiful future.

In the quiet moments of their daily life, as they dreamed about their future and planned their wedding, Joseph and Eliza knew that their love was the foundation of everything they had built. Their new life was a testament to their commitment to each other and the incredible journey they had undertaken.

With hearts full of hope and a future filled with promise, Joseph and Eliza looked forward to the start of the rest of their living lives. The love they shared was the beacon that guided them, lighting the way to a future filled with joy, adventure, and the fulfillment of their dreams.

The days leading up to the wedding were a whirlwind of activity and excitement. Joseph and Eliza threw themselves into planning every detail of their special day, from selecting the perfect venue to choosing the right music for their ceremony. They spent hours discussing their vision for the wedding, each decision bringing them closer together as they envisioned their future.

Their mornings were dedicated to organizing their wedding, meeting with vendors, and finalizing arrangements. They laughed together as they picked out floral arrangements, tasted cakes, and debated over the guest list. Every choice was a testament to their shared dreams and the life they were building together.

In the afternoons, however, their focus shifted dramatically. After a productive morning of wedding planning, they would retreat to their superhero identities. As the city's protectors, they donned their costumes and took to the skies, ready to face any challenge that came their way.

The transition from engaged couple to superheroes was seamless. Joseph, now fully embracing his role as Graveyard Phantom , felt a renewed sense of purpose. His powerful suit and newfound vitality made him more formidable than ever. Eliza, in her own costume that complemented his, had become a force to be reckoned with. Together, they were a dynamic duo, their partnership extending beyond their personal lives into their heroic endeavors.

One bright afternoon, after finalizing the wedding arrangements, Joseph and Eliza suited up in their superhero gear. Joseph's costume had been meticulously designed to reflect his evolution from Graveyard Phantom to Joseph Scott, with vibrant new colors and sleek enhancements. Eliza's costume, inspired by Joseph's, was both practical and striking, embodying her unique role in their superhero partnership.

As they soared over the city, their hearts were light with the anticipation of their upcoming wedding. The skyline stretched out beneath them, a canvas of urban life bustling with activity. They flew side by side, their movements synchronized, a testament to the strong bond they shared.

Their patrols took them across the city, where they responded to calls for help and intervened in crises. They helped rescue stranded motorists, stopped petty criminals, and assisted the authorities in maintaining order. The city's residents greeted them with admiration and gratitude, their presence a reassuring symbol of safety and hope.

During their patrol, they encountered a situation where a building fire had broken out in a densely populated area. The flames threatened to engulf nearby structures, and the urgency of the situation required immediate action. Graveyard Phantom and Eliza worked together seamlessly, using their skills and strength to control the blaze and ensure everyone's safety.

Eliza used her agility and quick thinking to help evacuate people from the building, guiding them to safety with precision. Meanwhile, Graveyard Phantom employed his enhanced strength and flight capabilities to extinguish the flames and prevent further damage. The teamwork they exhibited was a reflection of their deep connection and trust in each other.

After the fire was under control and the situation stabilized, they landed on a nearby rooftop to catch their breath. They looked out over the city, the setting sun casting a warm glow over the horizon. Their hearts swelled with pride and fulfillment, knowing they had made a difference.

Joseph turned to Eliza with a satisfied smile. "You were amazing out there," he said, his voice filled with admiration.

Eliza grinned, her eyes sparkling. "So were you. We make a great team, don't we?"

Joseph nodded, his expression tender. "We do. And we always will."

As they shared a quiet moment, the reality of their upcoming wedding settled in. Their commitment to each other, both as partners in life and as superheroes, was a source of great strength and joy. They knew that their love and dedication to each other would be the foundation of their future, both in their personal lives and in their heroic pursuits.

Their evening was spent reflecting on their day, discussing their plans for the wedding, and enjoying each other's company. The balance they had achieved between their personal lives and their superhero duties was a testament to their resilience and love.

The wedding day approached with increasing excitement. As Joseph and Eliza continued to prepare for their ceremony, they also remained vigilant in their roles as protectors of the city. Their dual life was a testament to their dedication and love, a balance they cherished deeply.

Their commitment to each other and to their city was a source of inspiration and strength. As they moved forward into their new life together, they knew that their love and partnership would be the cornerstone of everything they built. With hearts full of hope and anticipation, Joseph and Eliza looked forward to their wedding and the adventures that awaited them in the future.

The wedding day arrived with a radiant sky and the soft hum of excitement filling the air. The sun cast a golden glow over the city, a perfect backdrop for the celebration that was about to unfold. Joseph Scott and Eliza Billings were about to begin a new chapter of their lives, and every detail of the day had been meticulously planned to reflect their love and commitment.

Eliza, dressed in a stunning white gown that flowed elegantly to the floor, stood at the entrance of the grand hall. Her veil, adorned with delicate lace, framed her face, and her smile was radiant as she looked around at the beautifully decorated venue. The hall was filled with flowers, shimmering lights, and the soft strains of a string quartet playing in the background. Friends and family filled the seats, their faces filled with joy and anticipation.

Joseph, in a sharply tailored suit that complemented Eliza's gown, waited at the altar. His eyes were filled with emotion as he glanced back at his bride. The couple had chosen a traditional ceremony, with a few personal touches that reflected their unique journey and superhero personas.

As the music swelled, Eliza began her walk down the aisle, her arm linked with her father's. Joseph's heart skipped a beat as he took in the sight of his bride, her grace and beauty captivating everyone present. The guests rose to their feet, their applause echoing in the hall.

Eliza met Joseph at the altar, and they exchanged a look of deep affection, a silent promise of the future they would share. The officiant, a close friend who had become like family, began the ceremony with a warm and heartfelt welcome. The words spoken were filled with meaning, drawing on the couple's shared experiences and their commitment to each other.

After exchanging vows that were both touching and personal, Joseph and Eliza took each other's hands, their fingers intertwining. The officiant spoke the final words, and the moment they had been waiting for arrived.

"I pronounce you husband and wife," the officiant declared with a smile.

Joseph and Eliza shared their first kiss as a married couple, their hearts brimming with joy and love. The applause and cheers from the guests filled the hall, creating a sense of celebration and unity.

As they walked down the aisle together, now officially husband and wife, Joseph and Eliza felt a profound sense of accomplishment and happiness. Their journey had brought them to this moment, and they were ready to embrace the future they had envisioned.

The reception that followed was a lively and joyous affair. The couple shared their first dance as newlyweds, their movements fluid and graceful, a perfect reflection of their bond. The dance floor was filled with family and friends who joined in the celebration, their laughter and music creating an atmosphere of warmth and love.

Throughout the evening, Joseph and Eliza mingled with their guests, their smiles never fading. The evening was filled with heartfelt toasts, joyful laughter, and a sense of togetherness that made the day truly special.

As the night drew to a close, Joseph and Eliza stole a quiet moment together, stepping out onto a balcony overlooking the city. The stars twinkled above them, and the lights of the city below created a shimmering panorama.

"I can't believe this is our life now," Eliza said softly, leaning into Joseph's embrace.

"Neither can I," Joseph replied, his voice filled with emotion. "But I'm so glad it is."

They shared a tender kiss, their love illuminated by the night sky. The future stretched out before them, a canvas of endless possibilities and adventures. With their hearts full of hope and happiness, Joseph and Eliza looked forward to the life they would build together, both as a couple and as superheroes.

The wedding day had been a beautiful beginning, a celebration of their love and commitment. As they stepped back into their new life as husband and wife, they knew that their journey was just beginning, and they were ready to face whatever the future held with the same courage and dedication that had brought them together.

Chapter 8: Unexpected Guests

Joseph Scott and Eliza Billings were savoring their honeymoon, a beautiful and romantic getaway that allowed them to enjoy the beginning of their life together. They had chosen a secluded seaside resort, where the sound of waves gently crashing against the shore created a serene and intimate atmosphere. The days were filled with sunlit strolls on the beach, candlelit dinners, and quiet moments of connection that deepened their bond.

Yet, despite the idyllic setting, an unexpected and somewhat surreal interruption was about to disrupt their peaceful retreat.

One evening, as Joseph and Eliza relaxed on their private balcony, the tranquil ambiance was suddenly shattered by a peculiar sight. Emerging from the horizon, riding on a swirling mist, were two figures—both skeletal and ghostly, yet unmistakably familiar. The figures grew closer, and Joseph's heart sank as he recognized them.

"Mamma Scott! Daddy Scott!" Joseph exclaimed, his voice a mix of surprise and embarrassment.

The figures of Joseph's parents—his mother, with her bony frame and tear-streaked face, and his father, sporting an old suit that was cleaned and pressed for the occasion—floated toward them. They looked both slightly ethereal and intensely upset.

"Mamma Scott? Daddy Scott?" Eliza said, trying to hide her bemused smile.

"Joseph!" Mamma Scott cried, her skeletal eyes filled with tears. "How could you? We heard about your wedding from the Underworld grapevine, but we didn't get an invitation! Not a single one!" She sniffled dramatically. "Do you know how hurtful it is to be left out?"

"And let me tell you," Daddy Scott added, his voice tinged with indignation, "Mr. Skeletoleyes cleaned his bones, found his dusty old suit, and got it cleaned up. Do you know how hard it is to remove thousands of years of dirt from a suit? And for what? To not even get an invitation!"

Joseph and Eliza exchanged an amused glance, the gravity of the situation mixed with the absurdity of it all. Joseph stepped forward, trying to manage his feelings of both guilt and amusement.

"Mamma Scott, Daddy Scott," he began, trying to keep his tone respectful and soothing, "I'm so sorry. It completely slipped my mind to send out invitations to the Underworld. With everything going on, it just didn't occur to me. I didn't mean to exclude anyone. I assure you, it wasn't intentional."

Mamma Scott's tears began to fade, replaced by a softer expression as she looked at her son with a mixture of disappointment and understanding. Daddy Scott, though still grumbling, seemed to soften as well.

"Well, it's nice to hear that you didn't mean to be rude," Daddy Scott said with a huff, though his tone had lightened. "I suppose we can forgive you this time, but don't let it happen again!"

"Perhaps you could make it up to us," Mamma Scott suggested, her voice tinged with a hint of mischief. "How about a grand tour of your new life? We're very interested in seeing how things are going with our son and his lovely bride."

Joseph sighed, a smile tugging at his lips. "Alright, let's not dwell on the past. I'm glad you're here. We'll have a grand tour and make sure you get to see everything. And yes, we'll definitely make sure to send invitations in the future."

As the evening went on, Joseph, Eliza, Mamma Scott, and Daddy Scott shared stories and laughter. The mood lightened as Joseph introduced his parents to their honeymoon paradise, showing them the beauty of the resort and sharing his new life with them.

Despite the initial awkwardness, the unexpected visit turned into a memorable and heartwarming part of their honeymoon. Mamma Scott and Daddy Scott's presence, though unconventional, reminded Joseph and Eliza of the importance of family and the ties that bind, even across different realms.

As the night wore on, the family sat together under the stars, their conversation and laughter mingling with the gentle sound of the waves. It was a celebration of new beginnings, love, and the enduring connections that make life meaningful, whether in the Land of the Living or the Underworld.

The following morning, as the sun bathed their honeymoon suite in a warm, golden light, Eliza gathered her thoughts and approached the Scotts with a sense of excitement. Despite the initial awkwardness, the previous day had proven to be a delightful reminder of the connections that transcend realms.

"Momma and Daddy Scott," Eliza began, her tone bright and enthusiastic, "since you had to miss the wedding ceremony, how about we do it over again? We could have another ceremony, one that includes both my family and your entire Scott family from the Underworld. And of course, we can't forget Mr. Skeletoleyes. It'll be a celebration that brings together both the living world and the living dead world."

Joseph's eyes lit up with surprise and joy. "Eliza, that's a wonderful idea! I'd love to have a ceremony where everyone can be present, and it would mean a lot to my parents."

Mamma Scott's bony face brightened with a tearful smile, while Daddy Scott's usual gruffness melted into genuine happiness. "That sounds like a splendid idea, dear," Mamma Scott said, her voice full of emotion. "I'm thrilled to be part of such a special occasion."

Daddy Scott clapped his skeletal hands together, a gesture that, despite his lack of flesh, carried a sense of enthusiasm. "And I'm looking forward to seeing everyone gather. It'll be quite the event, I'm sure!"

Eliza turned to Joseph, her eyes twinkling with excitement. "We can have the ceremony here in the living world, then organize a grand celebration in the Underworld. It'll be a bridge between our worlds, a chance to celebrate our love in a way that honors both sides of our family."

Joseph wrapped his arms around Eliza, his heart swelling with affection and gratitude. "That sounds perfect. I can't think of a better way to honor both our worlds and bring everyone together."

Over the next few days, Eliza and Joseph, with the help of Mamma Scott and Daddy Scott, began planning the dual wedding ceremony. They coordinated with their families, organized travel arrangements for the Underworld guests, and meticulously planned the details to ensure that both realms would be celebrated in style.

When the day of the ceremony arrived, the air was filled with a sense of anticipation and joy. In the living world, the venue was beautifully decorated with flowers and lights, creating a romantic atmosphere. Eliza wore a stunning gown, and Joseph, now back to his true self as Joseph Scott, looked dashing in a tailored suit.

The ceremony in the living world was intimate and heartfelt, with Eliza's family and friends gathered to witness the union of Joseph and Eliza. The vows exchanged were filled with love and promises for the future. The blending of their worlds was symbolized by a unique ritual where they each held a glowing orb, one representing the living and the other the dead.

As the ceremony concluded in the living world, preparations were underway for the grand celebration in the Underworld. The transition between realms was seamless, thanks to the powerful magic that allowed them to bridge the two worlds.

In the Underworld, the scene was both otherworldly and enchanting. The dark, ethereal landscape was adorned with shimmering decorations that cast a surreal, magical glow. The Scott family and Mr. Skeletoleyes were present, their excitement palpable. They had prepared an extraordinary celebration, complete with spectral festivities and an array of otherworldly delicacies.

Joseph and Eliza entered the Underworld celebration as husband and wife, their arrival met with cheers and warm greetings from their ghostly guests. The atmosphere was vibrant and lively, a testament to the love and joy that transcended realms. The dance floor came alive with the rhythm of spectral music, and the air was filled with laughter and celebration.

Throughout the evening, Eliza and Joseph shared their first dance as a married couple, surrounded by their loved ones from both worlds. The sense of unity and happiness was palpable, and the celebration felt like a beautiful melding of their lives and loves.

As the night drew to a close, Joseph and Eliza stood together, gazing out at the combined celebration of their two worlds. The evening had been everything they had hoped for and more—a perfect blend of love, family, and celebration that honored both their past and their future.

Holding hands and sharing a final, tender kiss, Joseph and Eliza knew that their journey had only just begun. The wedding was not just a union of two people, but a merging of two worlds into one extraordinary life.

With their wedding festivities complete and both realms united in a beautiful celebration, Joseph and Eliza finally had the chance to savor their honeymoon in peace. They had chosen a secluded, picturesque location, far from the hustle and bustle of everyday life—a tranquil island retreat with pristine beaches, lush forests, and crystal-clear waters.

The first morning of their honeymoon was serene and perfect. As the sun rose over the horizon, its golden light bathed their private villa in warmth. The sound of gentle waves lapping against the shore created a soothing backdrop as they awoke together, their hearts full of contentment.

Eliza stretched and smiled as she saw Joseph beside her, his eyes still heavy with sleep but full of affection. "Good morning, husband," she whispered, her voice soft and loving.

Joseph stirred, his eyes meeting hers with a warm, sleepy smile. "Good morning, my love. I can't believe how perfect everything has been. This is everything I've dreamed of."

They spent their days exploring the island, enjoying each other's company, and reveling in the simple pleasures of their new life together. They strolled hand-in-hand along the beach, their footprints leaving fleeting marks in the sand. They dined under the stars, sharing delicious meals and heartfelt conversations.

One afternoon, they took a private boat tour around the island, marveling at the vibrant marine life and the breathtaking scenery. As they sailed through the turquoise waters, Joseph pulled Eliza close, holding her tightly as they took in the beauty of their surroundings.

"This is paradise," Eliza said, leaning into him. "It's everything we could have hoped for."

Joseph nodded, his gaze fixed on the horizon. "It truly is. And I'm so grateful to be sharing it with you."

Their evenings were equally enchanting. They enjoyed candlelit dinners on the beach, where the sound of the waves provided a soothing soundtrack to their romantic moments. The warm, tropical nights were perfect for stargazing, and they spent hours lying on the sand, talking about their dreams for the future and simply being together.

As the days passed, their connection deepened, and they found themselves more in love than ever. The tranquility of the island allowed them to focus on each other without any interruptions from the outside world. It was a time of pure relaxation and joy, where they could fully embrace their new life as a married couple.

One night, as they walked along the beach under a blanket of stars, Joseph turned to Eliza with a thoughtful expression. "I've been thinking about how incredible this journey has been. From meeting you to our wedding and now this perfect honeymoon... I feel like we've found something truly special."

Eliza smiled, her heart swelling with love. "I feel the same way. We've created something beautiful together, and I'm so excited for what the future holds."

They paused at the water's edge, the gentle waves caressing their feet. Joseph took Eliza's hands in his, looking deeply into her eyes. "No matter what challenges come our way, I know we can face them together. We've already overcome so much."

Eliza squeezed his hands, her eyes shimmering with emotion. "Absolutely. We're stronger together, and I know that whatever happens, we'll always have each other."

As the night drew to a close, they returned to their villa, wrapped in each other's arms. The honeymoon had been everything they had hoped for and more—a perfect escape where they could cherish their love and look forward to a future filled with possibilities.

With a final, tender kiss before they drifted off to sleep, Joseph and Eliza knew that their love story was just beginning. The honeymoon marked the start of their new life together, a life filled with love, adventure, and endless possibilities.

Chapter 9: Guardians of the City

Back in the city, the rhythm of daily life continued unabated. Yet beneath the surface, a new chapter was unfolding for the dynamic duo now known as Mr. and Mrs. Joseph and Eliza Scott. Their honeymoon had fortified their bond, and now, returning to their superhero roles, they were ready to make an even greater impact on their beloved city.

The sun dipped below the skyline as the city lights flickered to life. In their sleek new superhero costumes—Joseph's now adorned with intricate designs that symbolized their journey together, and Eliza's reflecting a harmonious blend of their styles—they prepared for their nightly patrol. The costumes not only represented their commitment to justice but also symbolized their unity as a couple.

Eliza adjusted her mask with a confident smile. "Ready to get back to work, partner?" she asked, her voice a mix of excitement and determination.

Joseph, his cape fluttering in the breeze, nodded with a smile. "Absolutely. It's good to be back, and I couldn't ask for a better partner."

With a powerful leap, they soared into the sky, their costumes catching the last rays of sunlight as they ascended above the city. The familiar sensation of flight was exhilarating, and the cityscape below sparkled with life and energy. As they flew side by side, their hearts swelled with pride and purpose.

Their patrol began with a familiar route through the city's bustling streets and quiet neighborhoods. They exchanged stories of their honeymoon, their voices tinged with laughter and love as they cruised through the night sky.

The city below was vibrant with activity—people going about their lives, unaware of the vigilant guardians watching over them. Joseph and Eliza made sure to stay alert, scanning the streets and rooftops for any signs of trouble.

Their first encounter of the night was with a group of petty criminals attempting a heist at a local jewelry store. With precise coordination and a well-practiced routine, they swooped down, quickly subduing the criminals and securing the scene. The police, accustomed to their assistance, arrived shortly after, appreciative but used to the duo's efficiency.

Eliza glanced at Joseph, a grin on her face. "Looks like we haven't lost our touch."

Joseph chuckled, his eyes sparkling with admiration. "Not at all. It's amazing how much more enjoyable this is with you by my side."

As they continued their patrol, their bond grew even stronger. They were a seamless team, each move and maneuver perfectly synchronized. The challenges they faced were no match for their combined skills and unwavering support for one another.

In a quiet moment, they hovered above the city, taking in the view. The city lights below shimmered like stars, reflecting the tranquility of their new life. Joseph turned to Eliza, his voice soft and sincere. "I can't tell you how much it means to have you with me, both in our daily lives and in our superhero work."

Eliza leaned closer, her hand reaching out to gently touch his. "I feel the same way. This city means a lot to us, and being able to protect it together makes everything even more special."

As they continued their patrol, their hearts were light, and their spirits high. They were not just fighting crime or protecting the city—they were fulfilling their shared dream of making a difference, while also deepening their love and commitment to each other.

The night progressed smoothly, with only minor incidents to address. As dawn approached, Joseph and Eliza descended to a quiet rooftop, taking a moment to rest and reflect on their night.

Their superhero life was just as fulfilling as their personal one. The city was their canvas, and they were dedicated to painting it with hope and justice. The thrill of their work was matched only by the joy of their shared life, and they knew that together, they could face any challenge that came their way.

With a final glance at the rising sun, signaling the end of their shift and the beginning of a new day, Joseph and Eliza stood side by side, ready to embrace whatever came next. Their love and partnership were stronger than ever, and as Mr. and Mrs. Joseph and Eliza Scott, they were ready to continue their journey—both as superheroes and as a devoted couple.

As the first light of dawn painted the sky in soft hues of pink and orange, Joseph and Eliza stood on the rooftop, taking in the serenity of the city waking up below them. Their night of vigilant watch had come to an end, and they felt a profound sense of accomplishment and unity.

"I still can't believe how perfect everything turned out," Eliza said, her voice filled with contentment as she looked at Joseph. "From our wedding to our superhero work, it's like everything's fallen into place."

Joseph nodded, his eyes reflecting the soft morning light. "It really has. And it's only the beginning. We've got so much ahead of us, and I'm looking forward to every moment of it."

They shared a quiet, affectionate moment, their hands intertwined. The city below stirred to life, unaware of the incredible partnership that had been protecting them through the night.

Eliza broke the silence, her expression thoughtful. "You know, I've been thinking about how we can expand our efforts. Maybe we can work on more community projects or even help with emergency response training."

Joseph's eyes lit up at the suggestion. "That's a great idea. We could really make a difference beyond just fighting crime. Being involved in the community in other ways could help us build stronger connections and trust."

They discussed their ideas and plans for the future, their conversation filled with excitement and optimism. It was clear that their shared vision for their superhero work extended beyond the nightly patrols.

As the sun continued to rise, casting its golden glow over the city, Joseph and Eliza prepared to return to their home. They landed gracefully on the balcony of their newly purchased house, the one that had become their haven and symbol of their new life together.

Inside, they enjoyed a quiet breakfast, the kind that marked the beginning of their routine as a married couple. They talked about their plans for the day, balancing their superhero duties with the more mundane aspects of daily life.

As they sat together, their morning meal punctuated with laughter and affection, Joseph felt a deep sense of gratitude. He looked at Eliza, her smile brightening his day, and he knew that this was exactly where he was meant to be.

"We make a pretty great team, don't we?" Joseph said, his voice filled with warmth.

Eliza nodded, her eyes sparkling. "Absolutely. And I wouldn't want to be on this journey with anyone else."

The day passed with a blend of routine tasks and special moments. They continued to balance their roles as superheroes with their roles as a married couple, each aspect of their lives enriching the other. Whether it was attending to city affairs or simply enjoying quiet evenings together, their bond grew ever stronger.

As night fell and their superhero suits were donned once more, they prepared for another evening of protecting their city. The anticipation of their nightly patrol, combined with the excitement of their ongoing adventures, made each moment thrilling.

In the glow of the city lights and the comfort of their shared mission, Joseph and Eliza embraced their roles with renewed enthusiasm. The city, their home, and their love were intertwined in a perfect harmony, and as they soared through the skies once more, they knew that together, they could face whatever challenges lay ahead.

With the city's pulse beneath them and their hearts aligned, Mr. and Mrs. Joseph and Eliza Scott continued their extraordinary journey, committed to making a difference and cherishing every moment of their extraordinary life together.

Joseph and Eliza settled into their routine of city patrols, their superhero costumes becoming a familiar sight in the night sky. As they glided over the city, the hum of their newly designed vehicle beneath them provided a sense of security and exhilaration.

One evening, as they soared above the illuminated streets, Eliza glanced at Joseph, her eyes reflecting the city lights. "Do you ever think about how far we've come? From the land of the living dead to this, our own little corner of the world?"

Joseph smiled, his gaze fixed on the sprawling cityscape below. "Every day. It's hard to believe sometimes, but this is real. We're making a difference."

They flew in silence for a moment, each lost in their thoughts. The tranquility of their flight and the beauty of the city at night were a testament to their hard work and commitment.

As they approached a familiar neighborhood, Joseph noticed a flicker of distress—a small fire had broken out in a high-rise apartment building. Without hesitation, they veered towards the emergency.

Landing on the rooftop of the building, Joseph and Eliza quickly assessed the situation. Flames licked at the side of the building, and smoke billowed into the night sky. People could be seen on their balconies, some attempting to evacuate.

"Looks like we've got a serious situation here," Joseph said, his tone serious. "We need to get everyone out safely and contain the fire."

Eliza nodded. "I'll handle the evacuations. You focus on controlling the flames."

With practiced efficiency, Joseph activated the advanced fire suppression system in their vehicle, directing a concentrated stream of water towards the blaze. Eliza used her agility to move from floor to floor, guiding residents to the nearest exits and ensuring they were safely out of harm's way.

As the fire began to subside and the last of the residents were evacuated, Joseph joined Eliza on the ground, their costumes smeared with soot but their spirits high.

"You did great tonight," Joseph said, reaching out to squeeze Eliza's hand. "I couldn't have done it without you."

Eliza smiled, her eyes shining with pride. "We make a pretty good team. And there's nothing like knowing we made a real difference."

As the emergency crews arrived to handle the aftermath, Joseph and Eliza took a moment to reflect on their work. Their efforts had not only saved lives but also reinforced their commitment to each other and their shared mission.

Back at their home, they took a well-deserved break, enjoying a quiet evening in their living room. The warmth of the fire in their fireplace and the comfort of their home created a stark contrast to the chaos they had faced earlier.

Eliza leaned against Joseph, her head resting on his shoulder. "Do you remember our first night together, flying over the city? It feels like a lifetime ago."

Joseph chuckled softly. "I do. And yet, every day feels like a new adventure with you."

They continued to talk and laugh, sharing their thoughts and dreams as they had so many times before. The sense of normalcy and the joy of being together made their lives feel complete.

As the evening wore on, Joseph turned to Eliza with a thoughtful expression. "You know, we've accomplished so much. But I've been thinking about what's next for us. There are so many more ways we could contribute to the city, beyond just fighting crime."

Eliza's eyes sparkled with curiosity. "What do you have in mind?"

Joseph's voice was filled with excitement as he spoke. "I've been considering starting a community outreach program—something that focuses on education, mentorship, and providing resources for those in need. We could use our influence to make a positive impact in more ways."

Eliza's face lit up with enthusiasm. "That's a fantastic idea. We could partner with local organizations and make a real difference in people's lives."

Their shared vision for the future filled them with renewed purpose. They spent the rest of the evening brainstorming ideas and planning their next steps, eager to expand their efforts and give back to their community in meaningful ways.

As they prepared for bed, Eliza and Joseph reflected on their journey. Their love, their superhero work, and their plans for the future were all intertwined in a beautiful tapestry of their shared life.

With a final, lingering kiss, they drifted off to sleep, their hearts full of hope and anticipation for the adventures yet to come. Together, Mr. and Mrs. Joseph and Eliza Scott embraced their roles as protectors of the city and partners in life, ready to face whatever challenges and joys awaited them.

Chapter 10: The New Horizons

As the days turned into months, Joseph and Eliza Scott became a symbol of hope and inspiration for their city. Their superhero personas, Graveyard Phantom and Eliza, not only protected their home but also helped to rebuild the community in ways they hadn't initially imagined. Their commitment to justice, love, and service continued to grow, and they found new ways to make a difference.

Their community outreach program flourished, providing education, resources, and mentorship to those in need. The program had a profound impact, and the gratitude from the city's residents filled Joseph and Eliza with a deep sense of fulfillment. They were no longer just heroes in costume; they were champions of hope and change.

One crisp morning, as they stood together on their rooftop, overlooking the bustling city below, Joseph turned to Eliza with a thoughtful expression. "You know, I never thought our journey would lead us here, but I wouldn't trade it for anything."

Eliza smiled, her hand resting on his. "We've come a long way, and every step of the way has been worth it. But I keep thinking about our future and what's next for us."

Joseph nodded, his gaze thoughtful. "I've been thinking the same. We've built so much together—our home, our superhero work, our outreach program. What if we took our vision even further?"

Eliza's eyes sparkled with curiosity. "What do you have in mind?"

Joseph took a deep breath. "What if we expanded our outreach program on a national level? We have the resources, the influence, and the passion to make a broader impact. We could partner with organizations across the country, addressing issues like education, poverty, and social justice. We could use our platform to advocate for systemic change."

Eliza's expression grew serious, reflecting on the enormity of the idea. "It's ambitious, but I believe we can do it. We've faced so many challenges and overcome them. This feels like the next logical step in our journey."

Joseph squeezed her hand gently. "And it's not just about expanding our work. It's about continuing to grow together, as partners and as individuals. It's about leaving a legacy that reflects our values and our love for each other."

As they contemplated their future, their thoughts were interrupted by a call for help. A new crisis had emerged—a series of natural disasters affecting several regions. Without hesitation, they donned their superhero costumes and prepared to respond.

The following weeks were a whirlwind of activity. Joseph and Eliza coordinated relief efforts, using their skills and resources to aid those in need. Their outreach program provided crucial support to affected communities, and their superhero work ensured that people were safe during the crises.

Through the chaos and demands of their work, Joseph and Eliza's bond remained unshakable. They leaned on each other for support, their love growing stronger with each challenge they faced. Their shared commitment to their mission and to each other was a source of immense strength.

As the crises began to subside and normalcy started to return, Joseph and Eliza took a moment to reflect on their journey. They had faced adversity, celebrated triumphs, and built a life together that was both extraordinary and meaningful.

One evening, as they relaxed in their living room, Joseph looked at Eliza with a sense of contentment. "We've accomplished so much, and we've done it together. I couldn't ask for a better partner."

Eliza leaned in, her eyes filled with love. "And I couldn't ask for a better partner, either. Our journey is far from over, but whatever comes next, I know we'll face it together."

They shared a tender kiss, their hearts full of gratitude and hope. The future was uncertain, but one thing was clear: they would continue to build their legacy, making a positive impact on the world and cherishing the love they had found in each other.

As they looked out over the city, they felt a profound sense of purpose. Their journey had led them to new horizons, and they were ready to embrace whatever the future held. Together, Joseph and Eliza Scott would continue to make a difference, inspired by their love, their values, and their shared vision for a better world.

As the days turned into months, Joseph and Eliza Scott's impact on their city grew. Their work as superheroes and community advocates had forged a new path for their lives, one filled with challenges, triumphs, and a deep sense of purpose.

Their outreach program continued to expand, touching lives far beyond the city's limits. They forged partnerships with national organizations, addressing critical issues such as education, healthcare, and environmental sustainability. Their superhero persona had become synonymous with hope and change, and their combined efforts were reshaping their world for the better.

One bright spring morning, as they prepared for another day of superhero duties and outreach activities, Joseph and Eliza stood together on the balcony of their home, gazing at the horizon. The city below bustled with life, a testament to the positive change they had helped bring about.

Joseph turned to Eliza with a contemplative expression. "You know, looking out at this city, I realize how much we've grown—not just as superheroes, but as individuals and as a couple. Our journey has been incredible, but I can't help but wonder what's next for us."

Eliza smiled, her eyes reflecting the morning sun. "I've been thinking the same. We've achieved so much, but there's always more to be done. What if we took our vision further, beyond our current outreach programs and superhero work?"

Joseph's interest piqued. "What do you have in mind?"

Eliza took a deep breath, her gaze steady. "What if we started an international initiative to support young people in underserved communities? We could provide scholarships, mentorship, and resources to help them achieve their dreams. We could use our platform to advocate for global change and inspire the next generation of leaders."

Joseph's eyes lit up with excitement. "That's a fantastic idea. We've seen the impact we can make locally, but taking it on a global scale could truly transform lives. We have the connections, the resources, and the passion to make it happen."

Their discussion was soon interrupted by a call for help. A new crisis had emerged—an environmental disaster that required immediate action. Without hesitation, Joseph and Eliza donned their superhero costumes and prepared to respond.

For the next few weeks, they worked tirelessly to address the crisis. Their efforts included coordinating with rescue teams, providing aid to affected communities, and advocating for long-term environmental sustainability. Their superhero work, combined with their outreach programs, demonstrated their unwavering commitment to making a difference.

Amidst the whirlwind of activity, Joseph and Eliza's bond grew stronger. They supported each other through every challenge, their love and partnership deepening with each passing day. Their shared mission continued to be a source of inspiration and strength.

As the immediate crisis began to resolve, they took a moment to reflect on their journey. They had faced numerous challenges and achieved significant milestones, but their vision for the future remained as vibrant as ever.

One evening, as they relaxed together in their living room, Joseph took Eliza's hand and looked at her with a sense of contentment. "We've come a long way, and we've accomplished so much. But I feel like we're just getting started. There's so much more we can do."

Eliza squeezed his hand, her eyes filled with determination. "I agree. Our journey is far from over. We have a chance to create a lasting legacy, to inspire others and make a difference on a global scale. Whatever comes next, I know we'll face it together."

They shared a tender kiss, their hearts full of hope and anticipation. The future was filled with possibilities, and they were ready to embrace it with unwavering resolve.

As they looked out over the city once more, they felt a deep sense of purpose. Their journey had led them to new horizons, and they were excited to continue making a positive impact in the world. Together, Joseph and Eliza Scott would forge ahead, inspired by their love, their shared vision, and their commitment to creating a better future for all.

The sun was setting, casting a warm glow over the city, as Joseph and Eliza Scott sat together in their living room. Eliza had been feeling unusually tired and unwell over the past few weeks, and Joseph had insisted she see a doctor. Despite her attempts to reassure him that it was nothing serious, Joseph's concern was palpable.

With a gentle but determined hand, Joseph helped Eliza into the car. "I just want to be sure everything's okay," he said softly, his worry evident in his eyes. They drove to the hospital, where Eliza underwent a series of tests.

The waiting room was filled with a mix of anticipation and apprehension. Joseph paced restlessly, occasionally glancing at Eliza, who sat quietly, trying to stay calm.

After what felt like an eternity, the doctor finally emerged with a reassuring smile. "Mr. and Mrs. Scott, I have some wonderful news for you."

Eliza's eyes met Joseph's with a mixture of hope and nervousness. "What is it?" she asked.

"You're not sick," the doctor said, "in fact, you're in excellent health. You're going to be parents."

The news hit them like a wave, and Joseph's face broke into an astonished smile. "Parents?" he echoed, barely able to process the words. Eliza's eyes welled up with tears of joy.

"Yes," the doctor confirmed, "You're expecting a baby. Congratulations!"

Joseph wrapped his arms around Eliza, holding her close as the reality of the news sank in. "I can't believe it," he murmured, his voice filled with awe and happiness.

Eliza, her heart racing with excitement, looked up at Joseph with a beaming smile. "We're going to be parents," she said softly, her voice trembling with emotion.

As they left the hospital, Joseph carefully helped Eliza into the car. They drove home in a state of euphoria, their minds swirling with thoughts of the future. The city outside seemed to shimmer with possibility, mirroring their own feelings of anticipation and joy.

When they arrived back at their home, Joseph and Eliza took a moment to absorb the significance of the news. They walked through their house, which now felt even more special with the addition of a new member soon to join them.

Eliza touched her growing belly, her eyes misty with happiness. "We're really going to have a family," she said, her voice filled with wonder.

Joseph looked at her with admiration and love. "This is the start of a new chapter in our lives. I promise to be the best partner, husband, and father I can be."

They shared a tender kiss, their hearts swelling with excitement for the future. Their superhero costumes and their efforts to make a difference in the world had led them to this incredible moment—a new beginning, filled with promise and love.

As they prepared for the changes that lay ahead, Joseph and Eliza knew that their journey was far from over. They would face the challenges of parenthood with the same determination and passion that had guided them through their superhero adventures and their shared mission to make a positive impact on the world.

Together, they looked forward to the future with hopeful hearts, ready to embrace the joys and responsibilities of raising a family. Their love had already created a lasting impact, and now it was poised to grow even stronger with the arrival of their child.

As the night fell, Joseph and Eliza stood hand in hand, looking out over the city they had protected and loved. The horizon seemed brighter than ever, filled with the promise of new beginnings and the endless possibilities of their shared future.

Epilogue: A Legacy of Love

Years had passed since that life-changing day when Joseph and Eliza Scott discovered they were going to be parents. Their lives had transformed in ways they could never have imagined, and the journey they embarked on together had led them to a place of deep love, fulfillment, and joy.

The house they had once dreamed of was now a home filled with laughter, warmth, and the pitter-patter of little feet. Their daughter, Emily, was the light of their lives—a spirited, curious child who had inherited her mother's kindness and her father's strength. She had a boundless energy that kept them on their toes, and a smile that could brighten even the darkest of days.

Joseph, once known as Graveyard Phantom , had found a new purpose in life. Though he still donned his superhero costume when the city needed him, his greatest role was that of a husband and father. The man who had been given a second chance at life had made the most of it, embracing every moment with gratitude and love.

Eliza, too, had grown into her new life with grace and determination. She continued to stand by Joseph's side, both in their everyday lives and in their shared mission to protect the city. But her heart was most full when she was with her family, watching Joseph and Emily play together, knowing that they had built something truly special.

As the years went by, the Scott family became a beacon of hope and inspiration in their community. Their love for each other and their dedication to doing good in the world had left a lasting impact on those around them. People looked up to them not just for their heroic deeds, but for the kindness and compassion they showed in their daily lives.

One evening, as the sun set and the sky turned a deep shade of orange, Joseph and Eliza sat together on their porch, watching Emily chase fireflies in the yard. The years had been kind to them, and though they had faced their share of challenges, they had always come through stronger, united by their love.

Joseph took Eliza's hand in his, his thumb gently brushing over her knuckles. "I never could have imagined that this would be our life," he said softly, his voice filled with wonder.

Eliza smiled at him, her eyes reflecting the fading light. "It's more than I ever dreamed of," she replied. "We've built something beautiful together, Joseph. A life, a family, a legacy."

Joseph nodded, his heart swelling with pride and love. "And it all started with a second chance," he said, his voice thick with emotion. "I'm so grateful that we found each other, that we made this life together."

Eliza leaned her head on his shoulder, feeling the steady beat of his heart. "Me too," she whispered. "I wouldn't change a thing."

They sat in comfortable silence for a while, watching their daughter play, the fireflies dancing around her like tiny stars. The world around them was peaceful, filled with the soft sounds of summer and the warmth of the evening air.

As the last rays of sunlight dipped below the horizon, Joseph turned to Eliza, his eyes shining with love. "No matter what the future holds, we'll face it together," he said, his voice resolute.

Eliza looked up at him, her heart full. "Together," she agreed.

In that moment, they knew that their journey was far from over. Life would continue to bring new challenges, new adventures, and new joys. But they would face it all hand in hand, their love for each other a guiding light that would see them through whatever came their way.

And so, as the night fell and the stars appeared in the sky, Joseph and Eliza Scott sat together, their hearts filled with contentment and hope. Their story was one of love, redemption, and second chances—a story that would live on, not just in their own lives, but in the lives of those they touched.

It was a story of a legacy that would endure, a legacy of love that would shine brightly for generations to come.

As the night deepened, the soft glow of the stars illuminated the quiet streets of the city they had sworn to protect. Inside their home, the warmth of family and love permeated every corner. Joseph and Eliza Scott were no longer just two souls bound by a shared past and a second chance; they had become the pillars of a life that was as extraordinary as it was grounded in the simple, beautiful moments of everyday living.

The next morning, the Scotts found themselves preparing for another day, but today held a special significance. It was Emily's fifth birthday, a milestone that both Joseph and Eliza had looked forward to with great anticipation.

The house was filled with colorful decorations, balloons tied to every available surface, and the smell of freshly baked cake wafted through the air.

As they watched Emily excitedly unwrap her gifts, Joseph couldn't help but marvel at how much his life had changed. The little girl before him was a testament to the life he and Eliza had built—a life that was rich, not just in heroics, but in the love and care they poured into their family.

Later that day, after the festivities had ended and the house had quieted down, Joseph found himself alone in his study. The room was a blend of his past and present, with old mementos from his days as Graveyard Phantom sharing space with family photographs and Emily's drawings.

He sat down at his desk, opening a drawer to pull out an old, worn journal—a relic from his time in the Land of the Living Dead. Flipping through its pages, he saw notes and sketches, plans he had made when he first realized he'd been given a second chance. But the last few pages were empty, waiting to be filled with the final chapter of this part of his journey.

Picking up a pen, Joseph began to write. He wrote about the life he had lived, the love he had found, and the family he cherished more than anything in the world. He wrote about the challenges they had faced and the triumphs they had celebrated. And he wrote about his hopes for the future—not just for himself, but for Eliza and Emily, and for the legacy he wanted to leave behind.

As he finished the last line, Joseph closed the journal and set it aside, feeling a deep sense of fulfillment. He had come full circle, from a man who had lost everything to one who had gained more than he ever dreamed possible. His second chance had become a life worth living, and he knew that whatever lay ahead, they would face it together, as a family.

That evening, as the sun dipped below the horizon once more, Joseph joined Eliza and Emily in the backyard. They sat together under the twilight sky, watching as the first stars began to twinkle above them.

Emily, curled up between her parents, looked up at her father with wide, curious eyes. "Daddy," she asked, her voice soft and sweet, "will you always be my hero?"

Joseph smiled, his heart swelling with love. "Always, sweetheart," he replied, his voice steady and full of promise. "No matter what, I will always be here for you and your mom. You two are my greatest adventure, and I wouldn't trade it for anything in the world."

Eliza leaned in, resting her head on Joseph's shoulder, and together they watched as Emily drifted off to sleep in their arms. The night was quiet, save for the gentle rustle of the trees and the distant hum of the city.

As they sat there, holding their daughter and each other, Joseph and Eliza knew that their story was far from over. They had built a life filled with love, hope, and purpose, and they were ready to embrace whatever the future held. Together, they had faced the past, and together, they would continue to build a future that was bright, full of promise, and defined by the love they shared.

And so, with the stars shining above and the world at peace for just a moment, the Scott family found their place in the world—united, content, and ready for the next chapter of their extraordinary journey.

As the night deepened and the cool breeze whispered through the trees, Joseph and Eliza remained in the backyard, content in the peaceful silence. The weight of the journey they had taken, from the realms of the underworld to the bustling streets of the living, seemed almost surreal in this quiet moment. The challenges, the heartache, the triumphs—it all led to this: a simple, beautiful life with the ones they loved most.

Eliza glanced up at Joseph, her eyes reflecting the soft glow of the moon. "Do you ever think about where we started?" she asked, her voice barely above a whisper.

Joseph nodded, his gaze fixed on the stars. "Every day," he admitted. "It's hard to believe sometimes, how far we've come. From Graveyard Phantom , the lone vigilante of the underworld, to Joseph Scott, husband, father, and protector of the living." He paused, turning to look at her, his expression softening. "But I wouldn't change a thing. Every step, every struggle—it brought me here, to you and Emily. And that's all that matters."

Eliza smiled, her hand finding his. "I feel the same way," she said. "We've been through so much, but I know that as long as we're together, we can face anything."

Joseph squeezed her hand, a silent affirmation of the bond they shared. They had fought for this life, and now they were living it—fully, deeply, and with a sense of purpose that went beyond just surviving. They were building a legacy, not just as heroes, but as a family.

As the days turned into weeks, and the weeks into months, the Scott family continued to thrive. Joseph and Eliza balanced their roles as protectors of the city with the joys of parenthood, watching Emily grow and blossom with each passing day. They shared laughter, love, and the occasional challenge, but always with the knowledge that they had each other.

The second wedding ceremony they had promised to their underworld family became a cherished memory, a celebration that brought together two worlds in a way that only Joseph and Eliza could have imagined. It was a day filled with joy, as the living and the dead came together to honor the love that had transcended time and realms.

Mr. Skeletoleyes had presided over the ceremony with a solemnity that was both touching and humorous, his ancient voice crackling with emotion as he pronounced them husband and wife once again. Momma and Daddy Scott beamed with pride, and the entire Scott clan rejoiced, their skeletal faces lighting up with happiness. It was a day that reaffirmed their place in both worlds—a bridge between the living and the dead, built on love, respect, and the unwavering bond of family.

As the years passed, Joseph fulfilled his promise to himself. He became the greatest superhero the city had ever known, his deeds becoming the stuff of legend. But more importantly, he became the greatest husband and father he could be, devoted to Eliza and Emily with a love that knew no bounds.

Emily grew up knowing that her parents were more than just her protectors—they were her heroes, in every sense of the word. And as she blossomed into a young woman, she carried with her the lessons they had taught her: the importance of love, the strength of family, and the belief that anything was possible if you faced it together.

One evening, many years later, as the family gathered around the dinner table, Emily looked at her parents with a thoughtful expression. "Mom, Dad," she began, her voice filled with the same curiosity that had marked her childhood, "do you think it's possible to have a second chance at life, even if you don't need one?"

Joseph and Eliza exchanged a knowing glance, their hearts swelling with pride at the wisdom their daughter had inherited.

"Emily," Joseph replied, his voice gentle, "life is full of second chances. Sometimes they come when we least expect them, and sometimes we have to create them ourselves. But what matters is what you do with those chances—how you use them to become the person you're meant to be."

Eliza nodded in agreement, her eyes shining with love. "And remember," she added, "no matter where life takes you, you'll always have us by your side. We'll face every challenge, every opportunity, together. Because that's what family is all about."

Emily smiled, her heart filled with the warmth of their words. She knew, deep down, that she was ready to forge her own path, just as her parents had done before her. And with their love and guidance, she would face the future with confidence, knowing that no matter what came her way, she was never truly alone.

As the sun set on their little home, casting a golden glow across the sky, the Scott family sat together, enjoying the simple pleasure of being in each other's company. They had faced the odds, defied the impossible, and come out stronger for it.

And as they looked to the future, they knew that whatever lay ahead—whether in the land of the living or the world beyond—they would face it with the same unbreakable spirit that had carried them through so much already.

For the Scotts, this was only the beginning.

Publisher & Author
B. A. Harris Publishing's
Email: b.a.harris.publishings@gmail.com
First Edition
August 20, 2024

Thank You for Reading

Dear Reader,

Thank you for choosing to read our book

Your support and interest mean a great deal to us at B. A. Harris Publishing's .

Your engagement and feedback are invaluable to us as we continue to offer content that aims to enlighten and inspire. Thank you once again for your readership and support.

Sincerely,

B. A. Harris

B. A. Harris Publishing's

Don't miss out!

Visit the website below and you can sign up to receive emails whenever B. A. Harris publishes a new book. There's no charge and no obligation.

https://books2read.com/r/B-A-ZISSB-UZZVE